Wild Boar

in the

Cane Field

Wild Boar
in the
Cane Field

A Novel

Anniqua Rana

swp

Published 2019
Printed in the United States of America
ISBN: 978-1-63152-668-8 pbk
ISBN: 978-1-63152-669-5 ebk
Library of Congress Control Number: 2019906677

For information, address:
She Writes Press
1569 Solano Ave #546
Berkeley, CA 94707

She Writes Press is a division of SparkPoint Studio, LLC.

Book design by Stacey Aaronson

Fireflies flutter
overhead
Purifying my pain
Cleansing my mind
Flies hover, stare
My Self
Proliferates into millions
I smile
Hovering above
Lost in the night-darkened sky
A breeze's kiss on my cheek
Throbbing dissolves in dew-dampened grass
Clammy warmth expands below
A dove's coo
Consummate passion
The morning sky stares down at me
One star dies, another is born
Clouds of gray
Shower ecstasy
Witnessing
Birth
Death
Rebirth

Stories whirled around me when I was growing up, embell-ished by the tellers' imagination. I thank everyone who took me along on their fantastical journey.

Most of all, I thank my family—Munim, Nabeel, Danial, my parents, my siblings, and generations of extended family on two continents—for their contributions to this story of men and women struggling to find themselves in a magical world.

I heard a Fly buzz—when I died.

—EMILY DICKINSON

Contents

SIX MILES LEFT

TWELVE DEGREES BELOW THE HORIZON

THE RED THREAD DISAPPEARS

About the Author

BEFORE SUNRISE

In the Beginning

My mothers found me a week after I was born. By then, I had lost a week's worth of maternal love that I would never reclaim, no matter how hard I tried. My birth mother must have thought she had left me with enough love to last till Bibi Saffiya and Amman Bhaggan discovered me on the train, wrapped in rags and covered in flies.

Bibi Saffiya isn't my real mother, and neither is Bhaggan, but when one of them nearly sat on me in the ladies' compartment on the train to the village in Punjab, they chose to pick me up and make me theirs. To most, that did not make either of them my mother, nor did it make me their daughter, but to Amman Bhaggan, that was all it took to belong.

"I know you never believe me, but Bibi Saffiya cried when she saw you lying there, covered in flies. As if she had felt the pain of bringing you into this world and the joy of seeing your eyes look into hers. Now she is bitter and old and has no one to care for her, but then she was young and frail. Her husband had just died, and she and I were returning from the city on a hot summer day to her father's village, banished from her dead husband's home by his sisters, who blamed her for his death."

Even at twelve, as I sweated in the kitchen, finishing my

chores, I chose not to believe her. Every time she told me the story, she adjusted it. Granted, they were only minor changes, but I noticed them. Bhaggan might not have realized, but I remembered details. In every telling, she had always been traveling with Saffiya when they found me, but sometimes it was summer and other times spring. The inconsistencies irritated me when I was younger, but now I chose to lose myself in my own thoughts.

Bibi Saffiya, the sole owner of this village, was recognized for her enormous house, encircled by acres of land, which produced everything we needed for all of our meals. We never bought any food from the stores in the city. It was all grown, or made in the village.

Saffiya was the only woman in the area who owned such extensive property without having to answer to a male relative. At least, that's what Bhaggan told me. The garden surrounding her house was filled with oranges, bananas, pomegranates, lychees, and guavas. In the fields closer to the house, ginger, garlic, and onions were harvested from smaller patches. Buffalo, goats, and chicken closer to the house were protected from the evil eye of neighboring landowners and the slaughtering ax of roaming bandits. And on the distant periphery, all the way to the road to the city, crossing the large irrigation canal, stretched alfalfa, wheat, and cane fields.

Despite my better judgment, I let myself pretend that I had been born to Saffiya. I imagined a prosperous life as her only daughter. I dreamed of inheriting the property and ordering my hordes of farmworkers to plant and harvest the crops, and to shoot clay pellets at sparrows when sweetened guavas enticed. When the neighboring farmers requested water from my tube wells and canals, I would charge them twice the rates and become even richer and more powerful. Like Saffiya, I would hire armed guards to deter cattle thieves and to shoot wild boar when the sugarcane ripened.

Amman Bhaggan's voice interrupted my daydreams, and her story continued, returning me to the kitchen.

"Flies up your nostrils, on your eyes. Whirling like dervishes at a shrine. You didn't cry. You lay there with your tiny fist clenching one of those wretched flies as if it were a rattle your mother had left you."

In the kitchen, Amman Bhaggan sat on her *peerhi* close to the clay stove, while Maria and I sat to the right on a long wooden pallet near the sole window, waiting for a breeze to dry our sweat-drenched clothes. I shifted away from Maria, and, as if by reflex, she moved closer.

If Bibi Saffiya was like my mother, Maria was like a younger sister to me. Younger by five years. We had spent most of the past seven years together. We even slept on the same charpoy in Amman Bhaggan's room. She was my shadow; her existence depended on mine.

For reasons that I could not fathom, Maria was persistent in hearing the retelling of my story. For me, the narration was a reminder that I had no parents. No one behind, no one ahead. So Bibi Saffiya had made me her daughter. That meant nothing.

But maybe Bibi Saffiya's discovery of me on the train seemed more miraculous to Maria than her own, desolate story. Maria's mother, Jannat, was crazy. She had killed her babies because they'd been born too early. At least, that was what everyone in the village said. Maria's elder sister, Stella, was a year older than I but had been afflicted by a leg-shortening disease when she was still a baby.

Amman Bhaggan, oblivious to the heat, continued my story as she threw the thinly sliced onions into the sizzling ghee.

"Bibi Saffiya told me to pick up the baby and throw the rag out of the window." The caramelizing onions sputtered in the heat.

"I never challenged her. The flies exploded in a frenzy. The rag might have been your birth mother's dopatta, but it was no cover for a baby. Your cord was still hanging off you like a piece of uncooked fat on cut meat. You were maybe a day or two old, or at the most a week."

Amman Bhaggan told many stories, but of all her stories, I hated mine the most.

My birth story was not one of hope and love. It was not one of family anticipation. It was of desertion. The woman who had held me inside her body, close to her heart, for nine months had chosen to abandon me in a grimy carriage. Had she looked at my face and decided I was not pretty enough? Had she heard my cries and decided they were not sweet enough? Had she touched my tiny body and decided it wasn't worth being covered with more than a rag? She had left me with flies as company.

Granted, Bibi Saffiya and her trusted maid, Amman Bhaggan, had wrapped me up and saved me, but for what? For this life as a nobody?

I sat in the kitchen filth, peeling a basketful of garlic to grind into paste for the biryani Bhaggan would cook the next day, to take as an offering to the shrine of Sain Makhianwala. I would try to hide the stench of garlic by rinsing my hands in lemon juice, but the odor, like my story, stayed with me.

My own tattered dopatta, stretched over my nose and mouth, made it difficult to breathe. The kitchen was melting hot on that early evening. Amman Bhaggan's recollection did little to relieve the oppressive present, as it only reminded me of my pitiful beginning.

For the past twelve years, I had worked hard to demonstrate the terrible mistake my birth mother had made in disowning me on the train. I would have been the envy of any mother. I helped Bhaggan with all the kitchen work, organized Bibi Saffiya's closet, color coordinating all her outfits, and cared for Maria, who was really a pest. I cleaned all the rooms and made the windows shine. The rotis I made in the tandoor were nearly as round as the ones that Amman Bhaggan made.

In fact, just the other day, when the maulvi had stayed for dinner, instead of returning to eat with his wife at home, he had eaten a roti that I had made, and he hadn't believed me when I told him I had cooked it. He had given me a coin and complimented me: "It tastes and looks just like the ones your Amman Bhaggan makes."

But Amman Bhaggan had ignored the maulvi's praise of my cooking, and now she focused on how Saffiya had saved me. Maybe she thought it made me feel loved, but one day I would gather the courage to tell her the truth about how this story really made me feel. Not today. She was in a better mood, praising our mistress, even though her lifetime of servitude was quickly demolished to insults if Saffiya was unhappy with the meal.

"Bibi Saffiya wanted to make you her daughter as soon as she saw you. She named you Tara. Like a tiny star amid the black flies." I knew the praise was to keep me peeling the garlic, so she continued her sweet talk.

"I wiped you clean, then took a small piece of cane sugar that I had hidden in a knot in my dopatta to stop me from coughing on the train. You sucked it as if you were six months old, not just a few days. Till the train reached the village station."

"You gave her the first sweet, so she's like you," Maria

chimed in.

Maria never knew her place. She liked to feign maturity beyond her seven years by referring to practices and superstitions that she had overheard the adults discuss, including Amman Bhaggan's having given me my first sweet, my *ghutti*, which had the power to transfer her qualities, both good and bad.

Maybe Maria was right. Like Amman Bhaggan, I could tell stories of Maria's birth if I chose. I was there when she was born. I was very young, and my memories are unclear, but I remember a year later how I carried her around as if I, rather than Stella, the cripple, were her elder sister. Maria's story isn't happier than mine, but she had a mother, Jannat, who swept the rooms and washed clothes; she had a father, Isaac, the gardener, who kept all the fruit trees fruitful and did odd jobs cleaning the yard. Jannat and Isaac kept the inside and the outside of Saffiya's house spotless. They worked every day, unless it was Easter or Christmas, and that was when I had to clean Bibi Saffiya's room.

Amman Bhaggan, like I, had little patience for Maria, but she was in a reminiscent mood and tempered her response.

"I hope her fate is better than mine."

"Better than Bibi Saffiya's, too?"

I scowled at Maria. "Idiot."

My response to Maria's comment snapped Amman Bhaggan back to the present. "*Chawal*," she agreed. "How could it be better than Saffiya's? No one knows Tara's lineage. Bibi Saffiya is the daughter of the great healer Khan Shahzad, landowner, village owner. Daughter of an owl. Stop talking nonsense, and tell your mother to clean the kitchen after I've cooked this meal. Otherwise, she will no longer have a job or a roof over her. If my fate is bad, your mother's is worse, and she needs to do her duty without being reminded."

Amman Bhaggan detested idleness and reminded everyone of his or her role in the housework routine. Life meant work to her, and death meant rest, so there was no need for rest until your time was up.

Of all the servants in the house, Amman Bhaggan was closest to Bibi Saffiya, so no one questioned her orders. She was everyone's *amman*, mother, and following her directions brought them all closer to paradise in this life and the next. Even Bibi Saffiya's relatives showed respect by bestowing upon her the title kept sacred for their own mothers or aging women in the family.

I don't remember a time when everyone didn't call her Amman, but then I also don't remember a time when she wasn't old.

Maria glowed with the recognition of being needed for a chore, if only to call her mother from her shack, set at some distance from the main house. She stuck her toes into the only pair of slippers she could find, mine, crashed the screen door behind her, and began shouting for her mother before she had left the kitchen.

"Amman, Amman, bring the broom and the bucket and the rag. Amman . . ."

Maria's screeching grated the silence she left behind.

My feet were numb from sitting for hours. Garlic peels were in my hair and scattered all around me. Garlic stuck under my nails.

Bhaggan concentrated on stirring the two pots on the dung and wood–fueled stoves. To her right was a smaller, recently clayed pot with goat meat and spinach for Bibi Saffiya, and to her left was a much larger steel pot, containing lentils. On one side of the pot were streaks of dried-up lentils from the previous three meals, embedded by the intense heat. Neither ashes nor dried hay could remove the stain. The pot would have to be covered with a thin layer of clay after this meal had been cooked. I reminded myself to take care of it before Amman Bhaggan noticed.

Now, as she sat cooking the evening meal, Amman Bhaggan blew on the dung fire and sparks cascaded around the pot, some landing on the spinach and goat meat as she lifted the lid. Despite the heat, an even warmer cloud of steam ascended to the makeshift chimney. The sweetness of cardamom and cinnamon, wrapped in the warm salts of spinach, subdued the now-tender meat.

To avoid Amman Bhaggan's seeing the unwashed pot, I snatched the blowpipe from her hand and blew at the fire under the lentil pot. The ashes around the dung cake separated, unleashing the searing heat of buffalo dung.

I coughed and eyed the pile of unpeeled garlic pods, and Amman Bhaggan started a new story, another one I knew well. At least it was no longer about me.

Bridal Palanquin

Bhaggan had told me many times why Saffiya had been traveling on the train the day they found me. Bibi Saffiya's husband had died, and they were returning to Saffiya's father's home after her husband's funeral—not long enough for iddat, the four-month mourning period for widows, particularly widows as young as Saffiya. I imagined Saffiya not caring that she had broken the taboo. Why should she? Her father had died just after her marriage, and now that her husband was also dead, nobody could tell her what to do.

Bhaggan was not like the other village women. She cared less for the restrictions of culture and religion. Bhaggan's parents could not have anticipated their only daughter's ill fate when they named her Bhaggan, meaning "good fortune." And she, like her mistress, chose to ignore the excessive boundaries.

"Bibi Saffiya's husband was her father's friend and was dying of breathing sickness even before they were married. On their wedding day, he coughed blood on his white silk handkerchief, but they all looked away. Her father tried everything: Greek cures, hakim cures, foreign cures. Nothing worked."

Bhaggan gestured to me to bring her a glass of water while she continued with the story and the meal.

"On the bridal dais, he perched stiff in his starched white *shalwar kameez*, his gray face framed with rose garlands." With her dopatta, Bhaggan wiped away the sweat rolling down her heaving breasts.

"'A corpse in his shroud,' they whispered. And Saffiya sat sullen, staring into the distance. They thought she had been drugged—something her father, the master of cures, concocted." Bhaggan gulped the water and burped loudly, and I returned to the garlic.

"We all knew her husband wouldn't be able to perform on the wedding night or even after. But they were of the same landowning caste. And Saffiya, without a mother, would be molded by her in-laws. I was packaged in with the dowry." She held out the glass for me to return it to the pitcher.

"Every morning, after her husband left their room, I was overwhelmed by the oppressive odor of overripe fruit that he emitted. That's when she started carrying cardamom to chew on, to reduce her nausea. I would help her bathe and perfume her with the *ittar* of roses and *chamelis*, making the room tolerable again.

"By midafternoon, when she left the room, her sisters-in-law had plenty to complain about on their visits every Thursday as they returned from the farmers' market. They were married to two brothers and lived down the street.

"'Look at the princess without a kingdom. Who is she, anyway, leaving her room when the day is nearly over? We spend our mornings cooking and cleaning, and even in the evenings we find time to sew and knit to stay productive, but she does nothing!' condemned the elder one.

"The younger would just criticize her looks: 'a princess with a flat nose and joined eyebrows.'

"They cooked the day's meals early to avoid the afternoon heat and couldn't imagine how Saffiya stayed in her room all morning, letting me, her maidservant, organize the house."

Bhaggan continued, "She looked through them all as if she hadn't heard a word. Even with her husband, she remained silent. She confided in me that she couldn't stand his existence, but may I die if I ever told anyone how much she detested that time. Her father would never have let her return to the village, so she endured her husband as long as he lived. Thankfully for her, it was not for long.

"'Why should I answer to anyone?' she would say to me when we returned to her room. 'My father owns ten times more land than their brother.'

"'Let them bark,' Saffiya would say.

"Of course, we both knew that her husband already had two children with his first wife. All of them had died many years earlier, but we never mentioned it. The day we arrived, I hid the photo that sat on the mantelpiece. The mournful eyes of the family long dead would be a bad omen for poor Saffiya. How would I know that her fate was already written in the blackest ink?"

It had been some time, and the pile of peeled garlic was finally larger than the unpeeled one. The aroma emanating from the pots suggested our work was nearly done, but Bhaggan continued.

"She never told me what happened during the five months when I left for the birth of Taaj, my second prince. Both Sultan and Baby Taaj stayed with their grandmother because I had to return to Bibi Saffiya. By then, her husband had already started to die. Within that year, he was gone."

She rolled her eyes toward heaven, as if to indicate that was where he must have gone, but shook her head as she began to admonish his sisters.

"They suspected I had brought a *taveez*, a death wish, from Saffiya's father. I suppose they thought I wanted Saffiya to be free to control the family fortune. I only wish I had that kind of power. Plus, Saffiya's father was a healer, not a killer. He would never have given me a potion for death. He was not like some of the other healers, who practiced black magic. And anyway, without a child, a son, which was never conceived, her husband's death would mean nothing to Saffiya, who was happier the day they buried him than when he brought her home in the bridal palanquin.

"They buried him in the graveyard behind the house, beside his first wife and two babies."

Realizing that the food would soon be ready to serve and the kitchen needed to be cleaned, Bhaggan turned to me, expecting me to help.

"Where is that bastard Maria? How long does it take to call her mother?"

"I've been standing here behind the door, and you didn't even notice." Maria swung open the kitchen door and wrapped her arms around Amman Bhaggan, half climbing on her sweaty back as she hunched over the cooking pots.

"*Ai hai*, you'll push me into the fire." Bhaggan didn't even look back at the girl but tried to shoo her away.

Amman Bhaggan covered her hand with the corner of her dopatta and pulled aside the lid on the lentil pot, leaning forward to dip the wooden spoon into the bubbling cauldron and pour a spoonful of cooked lentils into her leathered hand. Then she sucked at the scalding splatter. She poured another spoonful, licked her palm again, and wiped her nose with her dopatta. Then, without looking at us, she opened the first pot, pulled out a tender piece of goat meat, and chewed it to the bone. She then turned the bone around to slurp out the last piece of marrow.

Keeping her hazel eyes on the pot, she took out another

piece of meat, tore it in two, and gave Maria and me each a piece.

"That's enough, now. I have to start with the roti before Bibi Saffiya says the evening prayers. Her temperature rises the second she's hungry. You'd think all her prayers would give her some patience."

Bhaggan's praise for Saffiya was always short-lived, so I wasn't surprised that her tone had already changed.

"Amman Bhaggan, I'll knead the dough for you," Maria insisted. I raised my eyebrow as I looked up at her. Both of us knew the likelihood of Bhaggan's allowing her to do this.

"Daughter of an owl. You'll get me thrown out of the house. I don't know where your hands have been. Your mother cleans the kitchen, and your father empties the sewers. If Bibi Saffiya catches you touching her food, she'll throw me in the gutter for your parents to scour."

"Let her do it, Amman." I could always convince her. "And I'll massage your head for you."

"I should have had a daughter like you," she said.

I stood up, shaking the garlic peels stuck to the front of my *kameez*, and added them neatly to the pile in front of me, careful not to add to the disarray of the kitchen and to demonstrate the truth in her statement. I liked to prove that she was right and I was the daughter whom anyone would hope for.

"If only my man had lived a few more years. Every time he looked at me, I got pregnant. A year after Taaj, Maalik was born. I was three times lucky with my sons. The village folk cast an evil eye on my happy marriage. My husband wouldn't have let me die in this kitchen. He had made the payment for a plot of land, for a house with three rooms and a veranda. He promised me that.

"The morning the black magic of the villagers killed my

husband, he met Saffiya. He gave her some money. I saw him open our tin case and count large rupee notes. When he saw I had noticed, he hid them from me. He knew I would worry."

I had heard about the money business with Saffiya, but I couldn't understand how someone so rich would have cheated someone like Bhaggan of her money. Why had Saffiya not returned the money that Bhaggan's husband had given her for the plot? Why would she have let her name be tarnished?

"Even last week, I was going to confront Saffiya, to ask her about the money. But you mention money, and the gases go to her head and bring devastating pain to her muscles. I have cared for her all my life. If I complain now, she will say I am disloyal. But I tell you girls, without a man, your life is pointless. No respect if your man dies."

Bhaggan turned around to look at Maria. "Did your mother say she'd come? I'm surrounded by incompetents and impotents."

Wailing Babies

{decorative flourish}

The kitchen heat had taken its toll on Bhaggan.

"You take a nap on the charpoy under the *shahtoot* tree, and I'll finish the meal and serve it to Saffiya," I offered.

Maria didn't agree with my suggestion. She wanted to return to my story.

"But what about how you found Tara on the train, covered in flies?"

I gave Maria a sharp look to remind her to be content that I was trying to convince Amman Bhaggan to leave the kitchen and let her pound her sticky little fists into the dough for the rotis that night.

"What about your own poor mother?" Amman Bhaggan responded. "When she married your father, everyone thought that all the children would be like him—mute. But look at you. You can't stop talking."

Maria's father, Isaac, cleaned his surroundings in silence. He trimmed the plants and gutted the grass with a finesse unparalleled among the servants. Then he swept the front yard in the morning and watered it in the evening.

After every cleaning, he soaped himself at the stream that

ran behind the house, washed the dust-colored vest and sarong he had just removed, and replaced it with a replica. He then pulled a broken toothcomb from under a rock and straightened his tawny hair.

I would spot him from the kitchen window and pretend not to look, hoping I would see his private parts, but I never did. One day, I thought he stared back at me, but the window screen was too clogged with fly gunk. There was no way he could have seen me.

Isaac's wife, Jannat, swept inside the house and washed the clothes. Maria and I helped hang the clothes to dry, and when we had filled the line—Bibi Saffiya's undergarments underneath, covered by the *shalwar kameezes*, alongside the dopattas—to its capacity, we would cover the bushes with the washed bedsheets. Sometimes the dust on the leaves would mark the clothes. Then Maria and I would hold the corners of each sheet and stretch our arms as far and high as we could, dropping them with all the force we could muster, to dislodge the dust particles.

Jannat then ironed the washed clothes and left them in piles. Sometimes she piled them so high that the tower of washed clothes would sag to one side and I would separate them into smaller, more manageable ones.

This routine was soon disrupted when Maria was around three or maybe four years old, after her baby brothers died suddenly and Jannat started acting crazy. She'd forget to check the heat of the iron before ironing Bibi Saffiya's silk clothes, which would wrinkle and stick to the bottom of the metal, leaving a dirty brown smudge. Instead of cleaning the iron, she would rub the dark smudges of burn onto the lighter clothes. Bibi Saffiya couldn't stand this. She ordered Jannat to stop ironing, and I took over.

But that evening in the kitchen, Amman Bhaggan was not ready to relinquish her responsibilities with the dough. She refused my offer to finish the cooking. That's how she was. She complained, but, unlike Jannat, she never gave up her job. Instead, she kneaded the dough while she continued with Maria's story:

"Stella had just started walking when we found Tara and brought her home. Your sister was never like you, Maria. And then she got the leg-shortening sickness, and we thought she would die. After she recovered, she wasn't worth anything anymore. She couldn't wash or iron."

Bhaggan wiped her brow with her dopatta, added more water to the dough, and continued kneading it and telling her story.

"That's why Bibi taught her how to embroider. Now she spends her time embroidering bursts of flowers everywhere—"

Maria interrupted again—"If my brothers had lived, my *amman* would not have gone crazy"—explaining to us why her mother took no part in helping her sister.

We sat silently.

The village women talked about Jannat. They whispered stories about her born but unbirthed children—how she had thrown them into the canal, and how you could hear their cries if you walked along the banks at night. Amman Bhaggan told me not to listen to them, because they were all lies.

One winter night the previous year, Amman Bhaggan's son, Taaj, dared me to walk by the canal at night. I took Maria with me, even though I wasn't really scared. We stood on the canal bank in the moonlight. The water was black and bottomless. We looked into the water and saw two faces staring back at us. After a few seconds, I recognized them. The elder one smiled in recognition; the eyes of the younger one reflected our terror, which intensified as we heard the cries of a baby.

Maria squeezed my hand till it hurt, but I stayed silent. The painful cry of a drowned baby arose from the bush beside us. I bent down, and Maria continued to hold tight. Three baby kittens whimpered, waiting for their mother. Maria pulled at my hand, forcing me to follow her gaze. The mother stood a few feet away from us, eyes glinting, a dead rodent hanging from her mouth. I turned immediately and dragged Maria back home. Taaj was waiting for us, but we said nothing to him.

I looked at Maria, wondering if she remembered that night.

"But you, chatterbox—your mother wanted Tara to be your *choti amman*, a little mother to you."

This was one of Bhaggan's made-up stories. The reality was that Jannat didn't want a second daughter, and even though she could have fed Maria, she didn't want to. I carried her around on my hip, pretending I was like the other village women, only they carried one baby on their hip and another on their back as they busied themselves in the fields. But I didn't work on the farm. I worked in Bibi Saffiya's home.

Amman Bhaggan said I had been a good little mother to Maria, even though only five years had passed since they had found me on the train.

As always, the story ended with my beginning.

She returned to the kitchen business as easily as she had been distracted from it, calling out to Maria, "Is Jannat coming or not? Look, a dust storm has started, and then it will begin to rain and the kitchen will be a muddy mess. Go, my daughter— tell your mother to come soon, or both of us will have to an- swer to Bibi."

Garden of Eden

I t rained that night, and Maria hugged me closer when thunder struck. She kept waking me up but managed to stay asleep herself.

Maria and I both slept on the same charpoy in Amman Bhaggan's room. I must have fallen asleep when it stopped raining, but when I woke, I could smell the watered soil and the *chameli* buds mixing with the stale odor of morning farts in the tight room that the three of us shared.

"Where are you going?" Maria called to me from our charpoy, as soon as she realized I was no longer lying next to her.

"What's it to you?"

"Can I come?"

She didn't wait for my response and rolled off the charpoy to follow me. I could hear her bare feet squishing in the muddy puddle I'd just avoided.

Aside from the two flat pillows and bedsheets trailing on the ground, the two charpoys on the veranda in front of our room were deserted. Amman Bhaggan's three sons, Sultan, Taaj, and Maalik, slept there. They must have gone to the mosque for the early-morning prayers.

It was cool out. No flies, at least not yet. The sun still hid under the cloudy horizon but would soon emerge to crumple the coolness into a steamy swamp of sweat.

As always, I walked to the hand pump that spouted a cooling stream of metallic-tasting water. I splashed my face and rubbed the drool off my cheek. As I ran my wet hands over my hair to straighten it, I could detect the stench of garlic still under my fingernails.

Maria copied me, but I left her behind as soon as I was finished.

"Bring me a needle from under Amman Bhaggan's bed," I ordered, without looking back at her. Bibi Saffiya softened when I made a *chameli* garland and brought it to her before breakfast. Sometimes she pinned it into her graying and thinning hair. Other times she wrapped it around her thickened wrist and covered the two twisted gold bangles, remnants from her marriage.

Even though I had never witnessed garlands presented as a demonstration of love, I envied the movie actresses flitting across the black-and-white TV screen, dancing for their beloveds with garlands wrapped around their pulled-up hair or, even more tantalizing, dangling around their braids. I imagined myself dressed in a virginal white silk outfit, or in brash bridal red, my eyes lengthened with a swish of kohl. The contrasting white garland in my long black hair would sway as I danced through the *shahtoot* trees.

I convinced myself. The garland would be for me. Forget Bibi Saffiya. And whom would I entice with the enchanting perfume of the morning buds? Taaj had looked at me the day before when I was brushing my hair. When I looked into the mirror, he was staring at me. I wanted to tell his mother but decided not to.

But that would be too easy. I would cast my spell on Sultan. He would be entranced by the *chameli* aroma and my snakelike braid.

Now I was more excited than I had been earlier. But I would have to make the garland before they all returned from the mosque.

"If she wakes up?" Maria was always too concerned about getting into trouble.

I didn't know whether she was referring to Bhaggan or Saffiya, but I didn't care to answer. Out of the corner of my eye, I saw her run back to the room. *Chameli* fragrance filled my nostrils, which were still struggling to recover from the garlic stench. I began wrenching off the buds from the bush farthest from the entrance of the house, frantic to work on the garland.

When this house was first built, Saffiya's father, the herbalist, planted bushes and trees for his hakim practice. Isaac's father planted them, and now Isaac cared for them. That was what Bhaggan told us.

Some plants were used for prevention, others for cures. Bibi Saffiya would tell me the benefits of the plants that her father planted when I massaged her in the early afternoons, before she took her nap. Marigolds, which grew uncontrollably in the garden, cured the intestines and diarrhea, which Maria always got when she ate too many of the tangerines from the garden. When Isaac had problems with his liver, Bibi Saffiya told him to drink marigold tea. I made it for him for a whole month. I gave the same tea to Bhaggan when she had worms. Her breath smelled vile that whole winter.

Bibi Saffiya herself took two cloves of garlic, morning and evening, to cure her gas problems, which she'd had since I could remember, even though I would have liked to forget.

The flower of Maryam helped with childbirth and monthly

bleeding, but it didn't grow in this climate, even though Bibi Saffiya's father had attempted to plant it so many years ago.

Every Thursday, Bibi Saffiya would summon Isaac, who walked silently behind her while she ordered him to trim here and add manure there, as if he needed her directions. But he listened dutifully, eyes down, as if following a trail of ants. He knew what he needed to do. Amman Bhaggan said he took better care of the plants than he did of his own children.

I never saw Stella or Maria talk to him while he worked. I was the one who took him his meals, which he ate under the neem tree near the kitchen.

Now that I had reached the neem tree, I looked up toward the house and saw Maria jumping over puddles, as if she sensed my urgency. She held a red ball of yarn in her right hand, and in the left, she held up a darning needle.

"This is the only one I could find," she shouted jubilantly.

Chameli stalks are delicate, barely upholding their fragile white petals. Maria knew this, but she chose to bring the thickest needle in the basket. The stalks would be shredded by the needle that was to bring them together to make my garland.

"Do I want to murder someone?"

Maria rationalized her choice to me.

"It was dark in the room, and I was scared of looking under the bed in Amman Bhaggan's basket. This one was poking out of the big red ball of thread that she uses to sew the comforters, and I thought if you're making a garland with *chameli*, the red color will be best. You wouldn't want any other color. The red will look so beautiful with the white flowers. . . . Actually, maybe white thread would be better. Should I go back and get the white instead? I can—"

"Hand it over." Anything to keep the tranquility of the morning.

I took the needle and thread from her and squatted on a rock near the *chameli* bush. Maria wasn't as careful, and her *kameez* trailed in a puddle near the rock she had found, but she didn't seem to care, ever. We sat in silent meditation while I made the garland.

I had filled my veil with enough buds to make a garland for my braid. I shifted on my haunches and began threading the flowers. Maria, with no concern for the surroundings, sat following my every movement with her eyes.

I chose not to tell her that my plan had changed. She wouldn't understand. She was too young. And what if my plan didn't work? But I couldn't think that way. I would never get what I wanted if I didn't at least try. But if I didn't tell her of my new plan, she would never know that I had failed. I could pretend that the garland was for Bibi Saffiya, instead of for me.

The thick needle tore through the buds, and some fell onto the damp ground and shattered. Maria picked them up and stuffed one in each nostril. I stifled a smile, but she knew she had amused me.

I couldn't let her distract me from my goal, so I looked down at my task and hurriedly threaded the thick needle through the *chameli* buds.

The *chameli* bushes were at the entrance to Bibi Saffiya's house. The latch on the wooden door left a gap large enough for the cat to climb through. The gap defied any promise of privacy to the two-step entrance, encouraging secrets to leak in and out of the home.

I looked up briefly past Maria's short, scruffy hair, and the summer-dawn view from the entrance displayed the village's ten mud huts huddled closely to the left. To the right, expansive fields stretched to the horizon. Maria and I sat at the entrance of Bibi Saffiya's mud-covered opulence of many rooms that could have accommodated all the village families.

The wooden windows and doors hung loosely in disrepair, like their decaying, formidable owner. Each room seemed isolated yet connected to the next with multiple doors and windows. Halfhearted printed cambric curtains partially obscured the view to each adjoining room, authorizing eavesdropping.

The austere sequence of these rooms demonstrated for me the authority in Saffiya's own life, as well as her ability to control the lives of others. At unequal distances on the whitewashed walls of each room, a few unsmiling family portraits were testimony to her lineage and power.

In her bedroom, her parents' marriage photograph hung at a slight angle. I dusted it each morning, leaving it at that angle as I gazed at the young groom, Bibi Saffiya's father, who stared back at me, one hand pulling back strands of marigolds from his brow. His wife, Saffiya's mother, sat next to him, leaving enough space between them for a third person, who must have forgotten to join them. Her head was bowed low, a dopatta layered with a chador covering it, pulling it down, restricting her from making eye contact with the photographer.

Whatever I could see of Saffiya's mother was weak, unlike Saffiya. That's probably why she died when Saffiya had just started to walk. Amman Bhaggan, only a few years older than Saffiya, was brought in to care for her. She must have hated that, but I admired her for doing what was expected. I know I would never sacrifice myself for anyone.

The rooms adjacent to Saffiya's were storerooms bordered with large tin boxes stuffed with bedding for family members when they came from faraway villages. The sitting area, where distant relatives and farmhands gathered, was bordered with lines of century-old chairs and brocaded sofas. On one wall hung a blurry photograph of Saffiya's father's brother, who had died of the plague before he was old enough to get married. The mournful youth looked tragically away from the camera, as if foreseeing his early demise.

On the opposite wall hung a few ancient photographs of long-dead men sitting in a row in the front courtyard, or standing in a line near a newly purchased tractor. On the third wall were pages of an old calendar with religious calligraphy that couldn't be thrown away.

The other two rooms had charpoys around the circumference, separated by small wooden tables covered with starched white tablecloths embroidered in white by Stella. The remaining months of that calendar from ten years earlier bestowed color upon the rooms.

In the center of the rooms that made up the house was a mud courtyard with herbs in the corner closest to the outdoor kitchen, which was at the entrance. Maria and I sat cemented to the entrance of this house, engrossed in weaving the *chamelis* into a garland. When I straightened the garland to check the length, I noticed the mist rising from the stream that bordered the house. Just beyond that, a thicker layer of fumes emanated from the alfalfa fields, and in the far distance, the ghostly yellow cane fields blurred into the hazy morning sky.

The one-room mosque stood aloof, at a distance from the village, dismayed that the villagers, prioritizing work in the fields during the coolest time of day, didn't frequent it enough for prayers.

Once my garland was nearly complete, I adjusted my feet to reduce the pain of squatting for half an hour in an attempt to save my favorite, parrot-green *kameez* from the mud.

Maria sat cross-legged, gathering the fallen petals with her tiny hands, unable to hide her excitement. I could never understand why she was always happy or excited. Her pleasure was always exponentially greater than the event. She clapped with joy when she found a potato shaped like a mouse, or when her hands turned blue with the bluing agent for the white bed-sheets. I thought she might be a bit soft in the head, but Am-man Bhaggan said she was just a happy soul.

Unlike me, Maria was indifferent to stains from the moist-ened floor on her powder-pink outfit, which turned an ex-hausted gray because she hadn't changed for the past week.

Memories of her dead brothers shadowed her happiness, but a happy thought brightened even these sad recollections.

"These petals will look so beautiful on my baby brother's grave. Remember how he tried to eat them once, and you stuck your finger in his mouth to pull them out, and then he started crying because he knew you were mad, but you weren't, really, were you, Tara? And then Bibi Saffiya shouted from her bedroom to stop making such a racket, and then you said bad words, and she was going to put a burning coal on our tongues, but she didn't know we had broken all the buds. . . ."

She paused, looked up at me in panic. "*Hai*, I'm dead! We'll be beaten with shoes."

She was right. Bibi Saffiya's fury was unpredictable and unchecked. If she didn't notice, she usually didn't care, but if she chose to walk around the gardens later that day and no-ticed the fallen petals, she would let her wrath be clear imme-diately.

I wasn't going to let that deter me.

"Your mouth has the motions again. Will you stop talking for once? Of course we won't be beaten. Bibi Saffiya loves me like her daughter. She would let me sleep in her room, but she doesn't want you all to be jealous of me. When she shouts at me, it's out of love. How many times have I told you? We'll say buds blew off in the storm last night."

I convinced myself so I could concentrate on the garland.

Bibi Saffiya was my spoken mother, or mistress, depending on her mood and the time of day. She cared for me, her servant-child. She gave me everything I needed. I was like her—a woman who would make her own way in the world. I wouldn't need a mother, just like she didn't.

The other house servants envied our relationship and asked me to intervene when they needed a week off for a family wedding, or some money to buy clothes or to pay the village doctor to give them energy injections. At times I was unable to convince her, and at others I chose not to.

Bibi Saffiya was old, but not as old as Bhaggan. Unlike Bhaggan, she prayed five times a day and sometimes woke up for the later-than-midnight prayer before the morning prayer time, especially when the gases inside her troubled her.

Before each prayer, I would bring her hot water to complete the ablutions. Amman Bhaggan said she needed to purify herself because she couldn't stop farting. She cleansed herself every time she sat on the prayer mat.

The gases controlled her life. When I massaged Bibi Saffiya in the midafternoon, without warning, even the *chameli* petals on her pillow would start to wilt. I would hold my breath until I felt dizzy, and she would wake up and slap me to force me to continue massaging her.

The garland was nearly complete. I held it up to check the length. Maybe a few more buds would complete it. The last two buds tore as I attempted to finish my task.

"Oof! The fat witch hides all the best needles!" I mumbled to myself.

I looked up as I made the last comment. I knew my young friend well.

"*Hai* Allah! You used a bad word. Amman Bhaggan will hit

you with the fire tongs." Maria stopped gathering the petals to caution me.

"How will she know?" I gave her a threatening look.

"I swear by Eesah, the beloved of Allah, my lips are sealed."

"You know what'll happen if you do? You'll go to hell, and then the dogs there will tear your skin until you scream, but no one will hear you."

I had shocked her into silence. I added, "And cover your head. Don't you hear the call to prayer?"

When she faulted me, I distracted her. It was that easy. All I had to do was remind her of hellfire. She forgot she wasn't of the same faith as the rest of us, or maybe she wanted to pretend she was. Then she would be allowed to eat from the same plate as I.

Amman Bhaggan used the chipped blue plates for her own family and me, and the white cracked ones for Maria and her family. When no one was looking, Maria and I licked halvah from each other's plates and nothing happened.

I added the last *chameli* bud to the garland as the maulvi recited the last verse of the call to morning prayer: "Prayer is better than sleep!"

Without a loudspeaker, the maulvi's deep, rhythmic voice never ventured far from the one-room brick mosque. But in the morning silence, it meandered over the fields to the front steps of Saffiya's house, where Maria and I sat, tying the knot on my garland.

The morning prayer was the shortest of the five daily prayers, so, as we gathered the fallen buds to destroy all evidence of having broken the flowers, we saw a lone figure leaving the mosque. It was Amman Bhaggan's eldest son, Sultan.

"There's Sultan *bhai*. All by himself. Sultan *bhai* is so brave, walking all alone. Amman Bhaggan says you should never walk through the cane fields alone. Wild boar attack you and drag you into the fields—and you know, Tara, Stella says Sultan *bhai* works so hard. He gave her one of his old notebooks to press her flowers. Stella thinks he'll come first in his exams."

"Your sister can't even walk straight." Stella's body dipped when she walked, so she avoided walking. It was a burden for me, because I had to serve her dinner and tea every day.

Maria looked at me accusingly. She stayed silent.

I didn't try to hide my hatred for her sister. I stabbed the needle into the red cotton spool and continued, "What does your Stella know about notebooks? She spends all day embroidering tablecloths and pillow covers. She's never been to school, and she shouldn't take anything from Sultan *bhai*. Saffiya Bibi pays for all his books, and she'll give her two stiff ones if she hears that he's giving them away."

How could Sultan like Stella more than he liked me? I knew more than she did. Everyone said so. No one even noticed her sitting in the corner all day long. I could attract his attention and get him to like me before he would even notice Stella again. Granted my body hadn't developed to what I knew it would become, but my hair was long and thick. I could walk with my head held at an angle that made my braid sway across my buttocks and attract his attention. I would show Maria how easy it was to attract Sultan.

The Virtuous

n the movies on TV, it was easy. The heroine stood aloof under a tree or next to a bush full of flowers, and, like a fly to halvah, the hero gravitated toward her.

I radiated that magnetism from my seat close to the *chameli* bush. Sultan's lone, slightly hunched figure walked in my direction.

I fumbled to complete the garland before he came closer. I continued with my half smile, even though I had now pricked my finger enough to draw blood. I wiped it delicately on the darker flowers designed on the side of my *kameez*.

Maria stood up and began waving her hands to attract Sultan's attention. "Sultan *bhai*, Sultan *bhai*! We're here, near the *chameli* bushes!" she shouted.

This wasn't how it happened in the movies. Maria would ruin it for me. I was torn between stopping her and ignoring her and tying the knot to complete the garland.

What would the heroine in the movies do? She might have brought a friend with her. But not one like Maria.

Realizing that I wasn't sure how to handle the situation, I let events unfold without trying to control them. Maria ran toward Sultan, caught hold of his hand, and pulled him toward the *chameli* bush.

I busied myself straightening my clothes, doing anything

to avoid giving the impression that I was waiting for him. I breathed deeply once, then once more. I felt the *chameli* buds being crushed in my sweaty palms, and then a sleepy morning fly buzzed in my right ear. I swatted it away, but it lingered. It distracted me, and in my distraction, I felt a wave of calm overcome me. The fly buzzed some more and landed on the garland. I stared at it for a while. Its boldness mesmerized me. It sat there, daring me to swat it, but I chose not to.

So engrossed was I in this exchange that it was only when I heard Maria's one-sided chatter that I realized they were just a few steps away.

Sultan never said much. Bhaggan said it was because her eldest born was intelligent, like his father.

"People who talk too much think less. Silence means deep thoughts," professed Bhaggan, when referring to her eldest, of whom she was prouder than she was of Taaj or Maalik.

I didn't really care for any of the brothers. Sultan was sweet and shy and would help me sometimes when I had to lift a sack of onions or carry a jar of pickles from the store to the kitchen. Taaj made me laugh sometimes, but he was cheeky and I had to keep him in his place. I didn't pay much attention to Maalik, the youngest. He was slow and silent, always following Taaj's lead.

At times, I felt sorry for Sultan because he had a stammer. His two younger brothers entertained themselves at his expense. Their mocking angered him, and anger made his stammer only more pronounced.

Nearly every night, when Taaj pulled their shared pillow away from him, Sultan, half-asleep, would stammer, "Y-y-you idiot!"

And Taaj would respond cheekily, "How many idiots?"

Maria and I, sleeping with their mother, could hear this

exchange from the veranda outside our room. We muffled our giggles as we heard a fist hitting hard and Taaj crying out.

"Go to sleep, my sons," Bhaggan would mumble, drowsy from a tiring day.

So now there was silence in the garden, but the uncomfortable smell of egg, sweat, and coconut oil fragrance soon choked the *chameli* buds. Maria's mother, Jannat, said the sulfurous odor came from damp clothes. The boys all used coconut oil to keep their hair close to their scalp, and the sweat emanating from all three of them was always suffocating.

I took a deep breath to pay attention to my goal at hand. Somehow, this lone fly had given me a newfound confidence. I didn't think of the movies. I knew exactly what to do. I took my time arranging the buds on the garland.

"Look, I brought him to see the garland." I knew Maria didn't know why I wasn't looking up.

I felt pins and needles in my feet because I had been sitting so long. As I attempted to stand up gracefully, my foot tangled in my dopatta and I tripped forward.

As I straightened myself, I noticed Sultan's worn-out, open slippers and blackened toenails. I raised my eyes slowly, to ensure I captured his embarrassed gaze.

"Sultan *bhai*, I just finished this garland. Please pin it to my hair. Maria is too short."

He remained silent.

"Take a pin from my hair, thread the garland through it, and then pin it back again. I'll take care of the rest."

I maintained a low tone and spoke slowly.

His arms were fixed to his side.

I looked up again and then turned around, slithering closer to him, until he had no choice.

"Do it, Sultan *bhai*," Maria encouraged him.

"I just said my prayers."

"So what?"

He mumbled something about not touching a woman if you are pure from prayer, but then pulled the hairpin from the top of my head, taking out a few strands along with it.

I didn't flinch.

I passed him the garland, and he took it from my hand, making sure our skin didn't touch.

"Don't break the garland, *bhai*," said Maria.

I felt him fumble with my hair, the way Bhaggan had when she'd deloused me.

"That's it." I smelled the egg sweat and coconut oil moving away from me slowly. Then he sprang two steps farther at a loud guffaw from behind him.

"We're telling Maulvi that you were touching girls early in the morning," said his younger brother, Taaj, laughing.

Taaj, only a year younger than Sultan, was Bhaggan's middle son. Two years after Sultan's birth, Bhaggan gave birth to her third son, Maalik, after her husband's untimely death.

"Bastard. You'll tell on me w-w-when . . . You were the one who d-d-d-didn't come for the morning prayers," Sultan stammered, his voice raised a full octave.

"Your prayers are useless now." His brother laughed again.

"See, Maalik . . ." Taaj looked around for the youngest brother, seeking acknowledgment of having caught their elder brother at fault. Maalik, who was born of a grieving mother, had always taken some time to react.

Maalik's slowness worried Amman Bhaggan: "My forthright son. He has his father's honesty in him. He will always tell the truth, even to his disadvantage."

Taaj continued, "Amman thinks he's an angel, but only when she can see him. He does these things as if no one will ever know. I can keep secrets, but Maalik saw you too. He'll never keep this to himself. He'll tell Amman and then—"

"Quiet! N-n-nonsense, and, you, Maalik, don't you dare say anything to Amman. T-t-this is not your business." Spittle flew from the sides of Sultan's quivering lips, adding to his humiliation.

Maalik stared from one brother to the other, unsure of what to do. Taaj was in control of the situation, smiling at his brother's embarrassment.

"You're the one who'll get a thrashing. Or you'll get what you want, and Amman will arrange your marriage with Tara."

Fingers pointing toward the sky, lifting one leg and then the other, Taaj mockingly began the bhangra, the traditional wedding dance.

"Come on, everyone—join me. Tara and Sultan are getting married."

"No, they aren't." Maria looked at Sultan and then turned quickly to me for a confirmation.

Sultan moved farther away from me, fearing female contamination, and I moved closer and looked at Taaj as I did so.

Other, less confident girls would have been mortified, but I felt stronger now. None of them knew that Taaj's insinuations were exactly what I was hoping for. This was much better than the movies. Granted, Sultan was not the ideal romantic movie hero. He was more like the hero in a comedy—one in which the heroine would save him. I would do just that. I would save Sultan by the end of this encounter.

Sultan wiped the spittle from his mouth with the back of his frayed cuff. I could see he was now worried that he would be in bigger trouble than his younger brothers, who had missed the early-morning prayers.

I decided I would save him from his embarrassment. I

would share with him some of the confidence that was brim-
ming inside me.

"Really, Sultan *bhai*? Do you think it matters what Taaj
says or whether Maalik tells Amman?"

I pretended to be angry, first with Sultan, for overreacting,
and then with the two younger brothers, for creating a commotion. If only he stayed silent, he would stop making a fool of
himself in front of them. But there was no silencing him now
and, therefore, no way to save him.

Sultan's angry stammer worsened. "I'm going to tell M-m-
maa Jee that you didn't go to the m-m-mosque to pray. You hid
in fields instead. Have you n-n-n-no shame?"

Taaj laughed. "We're not the shameless ones. It's Tara and
you who should be ashamed, flirting in public this morning.
All of your prayers have gone to waste."

Maalik, who had been staring at me till now, looked away
and, following Taaj's lead, danced as if he were in a wedding
parade, stumbling when Maria screamed.

"Snake! Snake!" she cried, as she lifted her hand, pointing
toward the snake line in the mud under the bush. The *chameli*
petals folded in her dress scattered on the ground from where
she had gathered them.

"Daughter of an owl. It's an earthworm. Haven't you seen
them come out after the rain?" Taaj picked up the earthworm
from under the bush and threw it at Maria. "There's your
snake. Let's see if you die of a worm bite."

"Stop, or . . . ," Sultan shouted.

"Or what?" Taaj taunted him.

Maria started to cry, and I held her hand as we stood surrounded by the three brothers, Sultan stumbling over his words,
Taaj sneering at the discomfort, and Maalik choosing to look
above our heads as if the distant fields were more fascinating.

Sultan wiped the slime on his fingers onto his crumpled *kameez*. I crinkled my nose, and he noticed. He looked toward my shoulder, at the garland hanging from my braid.

Taaj's gaze followed Sultan's. He was not going to let his brother forget his slipup.

"*Ai hai.* The bride with Bibi Saffiya's *chameli* garland," he jeered. "She'll beat you, like she did the other day."

"My *amman* tells me to stay away from boys," said Maria, wiping her face with the border of her *kameez* while trying to save me from the infamy of another beating.

Taaj was quick to quell Maria's audacity. "Your *amman* has been with every man in the village. That's why she has a baby every year and then kills it."

We were all stunned into silence.

I stepped in front of Maria, as she cowered behind me. I protected her with my words. "Liar. I'm going to tell Amman Bhaggan, and she'll put a lit coal on your mouth."

"And then what?" Taaj took a step closer to me.

"She won't love you. She already thinks you're a loser."

Taaj hung his head and asked, "Who told you that?"

"I heard her telling Bibi Saffiya that Sultan studies hard and that you . . . you do shit!" I paused and then, for effect, added, "And Maalik is an idiot."

Maalik, who had joined Maria in picking the fallen *chameli* petals from the ground, looked at Sultan, expecting his elder brother to defend him from my vitriol.

He then looked at me, but my insult only grazed the surface of his feelings.

"You see," I responded, "the baby can't even defend himself. Your *maa jee* is right." He was only a year younger than I, but I felt emboldened by his inability to react.

I turned my stare from Maalik to Taaj.

Taaj, further betraying his younger brother, pulled the *chameli* garland from my hair and deposited it onto Maalik's head.

"Look, Maalik the idiot is getting married. Who will he choose, the sweet Maria or the sour Tara?"

"He can't marry Maria—she's not of our faith," I blurted out.

"So what? She's sweeter than you, isn't she?" Taaj laughed, pinching Maria's cheeks. She pulled away from him.

Maalik fumbled as he pulled the garland from the top of his head. "Sister fucker. It's you who wants to get your thing into both."

Taaj hit his brother on the head. "Say that again, and I promise I'll kill you."

Maalik kicked his brother, who, anticipating the attempt, retreated.

Sultan, now calmer, had been observing this exchange silently, moved closer to his brothers to separate them.

"You're not our father, so don't pretend you are," Taaj shot back at his elder brother.

"He's older than you," I added, "so he's like your father."

"Shut your mouth, bitch. He's only a year older than me. You have no father or mother, so who cares what you think?"

"I'll tell your mother, and she'll beat you with a broom. Then you'll know how to respect me." My voice was beginning to shake.

Sultan ignored this comment, picked up the bruised garland, handed it to me, and walked away. It was not like the movies. How had I not anticipated this ending?

Taaj snatched the broken petals from his younger brother's hands and threw them at his elder brother.

"Our *bakra*, the sacrificial goat. We'll sacrifice him on Eid day and throw a feast."

Sultan continued walking toward the house, not looking back.

I was determined that Taaj and Maalik would pay for my embarrassment.

Lies and Secrets

⁕

I picked up the garland, dusted it off, wrapped it around my wrist, and followed Sultan but kept my distance. Taaj and Maalik were no longer interested in me and ran ahead. And Maria rushed to the outdoor latrine.

By the time I returned the needle and thread to the basket under the charpoy, Amman Bhaggan had already left her room to begin making breakfast. I would help serve it to everyone after my lessons with Zakia, the maulvi's wife.

This was our morning routine. Taaj, Maalik, and I would go to the maulvi's house to learn how to recite the Holy Book from his wife, Zakia. That was the job of a holy man's wife in a village like ours. She taught the children how to pray, and he led the adults in prayer.

Saffiya paid the maulvi and his wife a stipend for coming to the village to bring religion to the villagers. They were outsiders, both from the northern hills, had fair complexions, and spoke a different dialect.

Maria, being of a different faith, didn't join us for lessons with Zakia. She loitered around outside their house, waiting for our half-hour lesson to end.

Maria didn't know that she wasn't missing any fun. Zakia

was a bitter woman who poisoned our morning lessons. If we forgot our lesson, she beat us with whatever was at hand—a broom, a hairbrush. If we were lucky and she was sitting too far from us, she'd throw her slipper instead and we'd duck to miss it. If anyone laughed, she'd throw the other shoe. When I complained about Zakia to Amman Bhaggan, she told me that her one regret in life was that she had never learned how to recite the Holy Book.

"When my parents died, and then during the forty-day mourning period for my husband, I wanted to recite the Holy Book," she told me. "I looked at all the mourners who were reading, and they were at peace, but I was not. Zakia might be bad-tempered, but she's showing you a peaceful path and paving your way to heaven."

"Will she be there too?"

"Where?"

"In heaven?"

Amman Bhaggan threw the stained dishcloth at me, and I caught it and smiled.

"No one likes her. Not even her own husband," I reminded her.

Zakia's husband, the maulvi, led the five daily prayers, hoping the village men would join him. The few village women who prayed did so in the sanctity of their homes. When a baby was born, the maulvi prayed in the baby's ear to welcome them to the faith. And when someone died, he led the funeral prayers. He also led prayers for the annual Eid celebrations and prayed when the crops needed rain. But, for all his prayers, he could not make his wife happy.

He never shouted at his wife, like some of the other men in the village, even if she sometimes put too much salt in the meal. He also kept bright sugar balls in his pocket and gave them to us if we greeted him with respect. And we never learned his name. We just called him Maulvi.

Maalik had tried to get more than one sugar ball by greeting him more than once in a day, but the maulvi was on to him and would only pat his oily head and smile at him and say, "May you have a long life, my child."

And we would all laugh at Maalik for being so naïve.

"Babies bring happiness to women," Amman Bhaggan said. "If the maulvi's wife had a child, she wouldn't be so unhappy."

Taaj echoed my complaint.

"She hits us with her slipper when we make the smallest mistake."

Bhaggan stroked Taaj's head in consolation but never gave him permission to stay home.

Unlike his elder brother, Maalik never complained. He made more mistakes and bore the consequences silently.

Sultan was the luckiest of the three. It had been two years since he had completed the Holy Book, so he stayed home to finish his homework before it was time for school. Then he joined Amman Bhaggan for ghee-drenched paratha flatbread dipped in cane sugar–sweetened tea.

After having studied the Arabic Primer for a few years, Sultan had learned how to read the scriptures with a melodious harmony that mesmerized us all, to the delight of his besotted mother.

The day he completed the Holy Book, Amman Bhaggan slaughtered a goat to celebrate. Bibi Saffiya gave him a brand-new one-hundred-rupee note. We had never seen such a large bill and could only imagine what he would buy with it.

He bought nothing. I know because I got to see it hidden in the tin box that he kept locked under Amman Bhaggan's charpoy, next to her sewing basket.

Six months after we celebrated the completion, I got to see the one-hundred-rupee note again, along with the rest of the contents of that box, the week my monthly bleeding started. Because of the bleeding, that whole week, I didn't have to take lessons from that bitter woman.

Amman Bhaggan handed me the rags to tie in place and said, "You know you can't touch the Holy Book now. You can't pray. You can't fast. But don't let anyone know, especially the boys. We'll make something up."

"That's not fair," Maalik complained to his mother when I told him I wouldn't be joining them for the lessons that week because of a fever.

"How does she get to stay home and we have to continue with our lessons? I'm getting a fever too. Feel my forehead."

Amman Bhaggan paid no attention and gestured to Taaj and Maalik to leave for their lessons.

That week, I got to stay behind and watch Sultan prepare for school. I covered myself with my chador and squatted at a respectable distance from him, waiting to see the contents of the box that he always kept locked.

"You mustn't tell Maalik or Taaj about what's in here," Sultan whispered.

I shook my head vigorously, excited that I would know something the others didn't. Instead of opening the box, he looked around and, seeing the door slightly ajar, stood up, walked toward it, and shot up the bolt to make sure no one else came in. My heart raced slightly at being locked inside the room; I wondered what Amman Bhaggan would think if she returned to her room and found us here together.

Sultan then lifted his shirt, slipped his finger inside the top of his *shalwar*, and pulled out a little metal key. He sat down again and pulled the lock away from the box to open it with ease. I kept staring at the lock, surprised that I hadn't noticed how small it was and how easy it would have been to pick open. But I didn't need to bother about that now, because I would get to see all of Sultan's hidden secrets.

I had been holding my breath until he opened the lid, and then I gasped. I stumbled slightly and steadied myself with my fingers on the floor.

This is it, I thought. I don't know what I had expected, but it was nothing as mundane as what I saw when I looked through the thin beam of light that filtered into the tin box.

On one side, his textbooks were stacked in a neat pile. On top of the textbooks was a geometry kit that he had bought five years earlier, when he had entered fifth grade. He took it out now and let me open it and look at the sharpened pencils, worn-out eraser, and bright green pencil sharpener with a mirror stuck on the back. A small wooden ruler lay next to another instrument, with a pencil on one side and a point on the other. Sultan showed me how to draw a circle, and let me draw some of my own.

"You would come first in school," he said to me, returning the items to the box.

I believed him but stayed silent. I knew I would never go to school. I was expected only to learn to read the Holy Book, and so the sole lessons I would get would be from Zakia, in her one-room, mud-covered home in the village.

Sultan chose the books he needed for the day and tied a belt around them. At a suitable distance from the books, a sad pair of white polished sneakers with gray laces were placed close to but not touching his two other outfits, a gray school uniform and a dull-green *shalwar kameez* that he wore on special occasions.

"They all think it's so easy," he confided in me. "I walk half an hour through the fields to get to the main bus stop, and then take the bus to school. There's never enough space on the bus, and we must hang from the sides or the rear ladder. Sometimes we climb up the ladder and sit on top of the bus, but we must hold tight, because the driver brakes suddenly. My friend nearly fell off the roof last week. I held him tight, but his schoolbag flew over the side. We shouted to the bus driver to let us off so we could pick it up. The driver didn't care. He just kept driving. My friend lost all his books. The schoolmasters beat him when we got to school."

Perhaps I didn't want to go to school after all, I thought. Or he might have been exaggerating to gain my respect. Then again, he wasn't like that. Taaj was a show-off, but Sultan was kind.

When Maria and I were younger, Sultan showed us how to write on the wooden tablet, a *takhti*, with a homemade reed pen. He wrote on one side in scrolling calligraphy, dipping the reed pen in a fuchsia-colored plastic inkpot covered in specks of black, the contents freshly mixed to a perfect consistency. He showed us how to write the Urdu alphabet—*alif, bay, pay, tay*—until he had drawn all the letters. I recognized some of them from our Arabic lessons with Zakia, but she didn't teach us how to write.

He handed the tablet to me, and I wrote on the opposite side, but when I handed it to Maria for her turn, she broke the pen and left black smudges on the tablet. We had to wash it at the hand pump and rub clay on it so Sultan could use it at school the next day.

Now, we squatted together on the floor near Bhaggan's charpoy, considering the tin box. I wasn't judging him the way his younger brothers did, and he must have sensed it, because he exposed his fears.

"This year is my last chance to take the final exams. I have already taken them twice before. Amman keeps saying I am smart, like my father, but he never went to school. I've been in the same grade for three years now. I can never remember the dates of the wars for freedom, and sums gets more difficult every year. I don't know what will happen if I fail again."

He wanted me to feel sorry for him, but I couldn't. Every day, he got to leave home. He got to take the bus. He had a box full of his own books. He didn't have to stay and help in the kitchen, and he didn't have to sit with the younger kids to rock back and forth on the same primer I had read for the last two years.

I didn't care to stay in the village my whole life. I would leave it. I wasn't sure what I would do once I had left, but I was confident that there was a lot more to seek than the people around me and my thoughts within.

Dissonant Harmonies

On the day I made the *chameli* garland, my monthly bleeding had ended, which meant I had to go to the maulvi's house, instead of watching Sultan prepare for school.

As with all the homes in the village, the smell of burning dung emanated from Zakia's kitchen, a pyre to buffalo waste. Before we reached the front door, we could detect the odor, but the pungent smoke comforted me more than Zakia, in her unfathomable rigidity.

In the courtyard, close to the front door, Zakia sat on a low stool at her outdoor kitchen. The two clay stoves that made up her kitchen were built in the corner of the veranda. At some distance was the pump that served as the sole source of water in the one-room house.

Her two other students for the morning lessons, Hamida and Nafissa, twin sisters from next door, were preparing the morning meal. They sat close to Zakia. Hamida rocked as she kneaded the dough to make rotis, and Nafissa sliced the onions to prepare the main meal later that day.

Hamida and Nafissa cleaned Zakia's house, washed her clothes, swept her floors, and cooked her meals in exchange for her teaching them to read, for which they were beholden to her. Their parents and grandparents had never had the opportunity or the reason to learn how to read the Holy Book, or any other book, for that matter.

Like Taaj, Maalik, and I, the adults must have chosen ways to avoid learning from a teacher like ours when they were young. We slipped into the front courtyard without Zakia's noticing us. If we stood silent for half an hour, she would not expect to teach us, and we would leave when the time was up.

The early-morning shadows of the lone lemon tree in the front courtyard camouflaged us for a few minutes. I stood close enough to see her wrinkled clothes and unbrushed braid, covered hurriedly with a blue dopatta. Zakia was preoccupied, the frown on her forehead holding tight to thoughts that she would never share.

She rolled up the sleeve of her right arm and then rolled it back down again, sensing Hamida and Nafissa halting their dough making and onion peeling to stare at the bright scars on her taut left wrist, contrasting with three green glass bangles.

As she looked away from them, she saw the three of us in the doorway and spoke harshly. "Where were you all buried this morning? When the maulvi comes, you boys will get a beating."

Then she looked at me.

"And you, daughter of a nabob, what's with the flowers on your wrist? You think you're a movie star?"

We didn't respond but took special care to straighten our shoes as we took them off to sit on the reed mat in the courtyard.

"Yes, you—princess without a state! Where have you been?"

I straightened myself and pulled my head higher, my bruise barely healed from the time she had hit me with a coal catcher for laughing when she'd stumbled. I wouldn't let that happen again.

Under my glare, she busied herself stirring the onions in the oil. She hunched on the stool, covered with ashes that Hamida had just blown over her while helping to build the fire. She looked old, and I felt even more beautiful. But I didn't have enough feelings to feel sorry for her. She was quick to remind me why I shouldn't.

"You didn't throw out all the garbage yesterday. Look at that corner, piled with filth, covered in flies," she scolded Hamida.

Amman Bhaggan scolded me about keeping the place clean too, but it didn't bother me as it did when it came from Zakia. Would she sound different if she had her own child? I, the motherless child, and she, the childless mother. Did we behave differently because of what we lacked? Would I have had more respect if my mother had taught me? Would she have had more love if she'd had a child?

Unable to stop myself, I blurted out, "You only talk to her like that because you know her mother is afraid to say anything to you."

I glanced at Hamida to see if she realized that I was trying to protect her, but she had already moved on to cleaning the clay stove—an unnecessary task for an outdoor stove that would capture dust regardless of how often it was cleaned. Everything here was covered in dust. And the dust was covered with a layer of flies.

I attempted a deeper stab: "No wonder Allah doesn't grant you a baby. He knows you wouldn't care for one."

"How dare you!" she yelled. "After all I do for all you brainless idiots. This is how you repay me? Get out!"

Then she took off her slipper and threw it at me, and I

ducked, and it flew past, barely missing the maulvi, who, having returned from the mosque, stood in the doorway.

I covered my face with my chador to hide my smile and waited for the maulvi to explode, but before he could react, the sound of raucous movie music emanated from the house next door: "When you whisper my name, I die in ecstasy."

It was the soundtrack of one of the most popular movies of the time, and it drowned out all other noise.

Just then, Zakia fainted, toppling off her perch on the stool. She had a habit of reacting to loud noises like that.

Hamida and Nafissa rushed to her.

"Bring her some water!" one said.

"No, rub her feet," the other suggested.

The two boys jumped up from their lessons, pleased at the diversion. "What happened to her?" Maalik asked.

"It's the loud music," Hamida whispered. "Our father can't hear, so he keeps the volume up, and she faints every time he does that."

Taaj raised an eyebrow and grinned, though he stayed silent, since the maulvi still stood in the doorway.

Now he moved closer to his wife, but we knew he would never touch her in front of us.

"Help your *khala jaan*," he said to the girls, sitting close to her.

Hamida started rubbing Zakia's feet and gestured to her sister. "Help me straighten her. She's too heavy for me to move."

The twins tried to bring their teacher back to consciousness. They still hadn't started their lessons and would have to memorize the page before they left. Then they had to clean the lentils too.

Zakia came to and pointed weakly toward a glass of water on the table in the corner.

"Hand me that glass. The maulvi blessed that water. It'll give me the strength I need to handle my trauma."

The maulvi reached down to retrieve his wife's slipper, which lay on the ground nearby. He lifted it and gently placed it at the edge of her stool.

"And why is Tara standing, doing nothing?" He looked at me.

I looked directly at him, aware of his half-shut eye, and said, "I want to read the Holy Book with melody, like Sultan."

"Only boys can do that," he responded in a subdued voice, like when he explained to Sultan the times for prayer. I listened carefully to what he told the boys. Their lessons were so much more interesting than my mere memorizations in a language I would never understand.

"The first call is before sunrise. The second is in the afternoon—the time of necessity, as it is called. The third is when there's enough time for a man to walk six miles before the sun sets," he explained to Sultan, anticipating that, one day, Sultan might take on the role of village maulvi himself. I knew that I, even as a grown woman, would be expected only to follow the call to prayer, never to lead it, as a man would.

"The fourth is when the sun is twelve degrees below the horizon."

I never asked him what he meant by that. Maybe now I would.

"The fifth, and final, is when the red thread of the sun disappears," he ended.

If I couldn't make the call to prayer, I would be sure I could read the Holy Book with the harmony I'd heard when Sultan had learned.

"But why can't I? I've completed the primer and have memorized the prayers Bibi Zakia taught me. Why can't I read in harmony, like the boys?"

"Because your *massi* Zakia here doesn't know how to read like that, so she can't teach you."

I felt an even stronger urge now that I knew that Zakia didn't know how to read that way.

"Then *you* teach me."

I wanted to take down the bride-red, brocade-covered Holy Book and caress it lovingly in my hands. I would unwrap it and place it delicately on the intricately carved wooden reading stand. Then, very deliberately, I would open it at the silk bookmark and luxuriate on the green, black, and white Arabic script, with the delicate translation below. Then, like Sultan, I would place my right-hand pointer on the page, take a deep breath, and begin reciting what I read.

The maulvi would follow my finger as it underlined each word, scrutinizing for blunders. His left eye, permanently shut with an ax mark, would move as if it could see.

Neither of us would completely understand what I read. It was in Arabic, and neither of us knew it, but it sounded so beautiful.

As he followed my finger on the page, I would not dare look at his face. Maybe if I could look into his unseeing eye, I would glimpse the memory of despair about a younger son with no option but to teach reluctant children how to decipher this mysterious script from centuries earlier.

I would see the son forced to marry his older cousin because no other suitor was reaching out to her. She came with a dowry of furniture for two rooms, just enough to fill the home he would receive in the village where he chose to lead in prayer.

His wife would teach the village girls, like Hamida and Nafissa, who spent the afternoon cooking and cleaning in exchange for a half-hour lesson of reading the primer to the book each day.

As if realizing my wish, the maulvi sat on the charpoy on the veranda and told me to sit next to him.

"Follow me," he said.

And I did. I inhaled till I felt dizzy, squeezed my larynx, and began with the best of intentions:

Aoozobillahe minishaita nirajemm: I seek refuge from Allah from the outcast Satan!

Amman Bhaggan was right. Reading the Holy Book was peaceful. Each verse rhymed with the next, creating a familiar harmony that helped me forget the hawk-eyed maulvi following my every note.

I feared the maulvi's gaze, even though I had no reason to. Nothing he had done had caused me harm, but I knew what he did. I had heard everything that his wife had shared with Bibi Saffiya and Amman Bhaggan. In hushed voices, she had told them how he forced himself on her to create a child that her barren womb would never bear. The violent secondhand memory had seared my mind. I hurriedly finished the verse, not sure that I had the strength to continue my pursuit of finding my way into a world designated for men.

Glass and Marbles

The maulvi mumbled a *shabash* for my first attempt at reading the Holy Book with harmony, but I didn't think my lessons would continue. I sat with my hands in my lap, unsure of what to do next, and he spoke softly.

"Leave it here." He gestured to the book. "I need to read it before I eat. Go home now."

I gave a perfunctory salaam to Zakia, who was now upright, with the two girls still hovering around her. The boys had already left. They had to go to school. I pulled my chador tightly over my head and rushed toward the front door.

Beams of sunlight reflected off the marbles in Maria's right hand as she juggled them and then caught all three in her left hand. Her tiny fingers strained to keep them from falling onto the dusty pathway just outside the maulvi's house.

I stumbled across the maulvi's doorstep toward my friend, glad to be distracted by her dexterity. As if sensing an audience, she looked up and caught my admiration. She embraced me with her warm smile.

Abandoning her pride in having caught the marbles, she praised me instead.

"Your recitation, it sounded so beautiful. How did you convince Maulvi to teach you?"

With ease, I projected my accomplishments for Maria's veneration, and, with the same ease, she embraced my explanation. I badly needed to comfort myself by maintaining control of the situation, even if my perception was a skewed interpretation of reality.

"He had no choice this time. I wasn't going to let him go."

Still feeling uneasy, I switched the focus to her, declaring, "You should be happy you only have to go to the church on Sunday. I must do a lot more work than you. I have the morning lessons, and then I'm supposed to pray five times a day. You have it much easier than me, sitting juggling marbles on the streets."

"Did you see how I caught all the marbles in one hand?" She stood up, smiling, with her hands on her hips.

But I felt my self-control returning, and so I ignored her question. Sensing the putdown, with a turn of her head, Maria signaled her impatience, but I was her match.

"If I had time like you, I would have done better than that. And I can still beat you at hopscotch." I didn't want the situation to slip out of my control.

"But you're taller than me," she mumbled, clarifying why I could jump across the big squares that we both knew I drew large enough to make her stumble.

Maria's smiling lips straightened, and she turned to walk in the opposite direction. I didn't want her to know that I would rather have spent with her the half hour I'd been at the maulvi's house.

Instead I pulled my dopatta around my head to shift the moth hole to one side and hide it in the folds, pulled my shoulders back, and lifted my still-developing chest. I would never admit to Maria that I sought out her company to build my confidence. I decided to follow her but picked up speed so it seemed as if I were leading the way. I would join her in helping her sister, Stella, and take her to Saffiya's home.

We walked past the mud houses, and I pulled her aside when she wanted to step on dog shit in the middle of the road. We could hear the village sounds of chickens, cows, and the tractor humming in the distance. Somehow, our silence was louder than those sounds.

As Maria's parents' one-room home came into view, the high-pitched, frenzied screeching of Jannat, Maria's mother, warned us to slow down. As we got closer, we realized Stella was the focus of her ire.

"I swear, my mouth fills with bile. Even your father doesn't smell that bad. Can't you smell the foul stench of egg? And why does he stare at you? What does he see in a cripple like you? I tell you, he is deranged. Crazy."

Jannat's breathlessness and the swish of the broom as she berated her daughter Stella indicated that she was busy sweeping the one-room hut.

"Sultan is just like his father. The old hag Bhaggan thinks her husband was perfect, but he wasn't. The whole village knows his reality."

Maria slipped her hand into mine as we moved closer to the door. I had never heard anyone disparage Bhaggan's husband, or Sultan, for that matter. Had Jannat always disapproved of them, or was this one of her fits that would force Maria to return to me for company?

"Bhaggan's husband came and went to the main house as if he belonged. And now his son does the same. Why does he go into the room where you sit to do your embroidery? I've seen him stare at you when you limp by him."

I was surprised to hear her criticism. When had Sultan shown so much interest in Stella? Jannat was on a rampage.

"Quiet boys are more dangerous. I don't know his intentions, but you keep your distance from him."

I was outraged that Jannat, the crazy woman, was maligning Sultan. Why would he be attracted to Stella? He had confided in me, shared his fears, and now Jannat was insinuating that he preferred Stella, not me. Had Maria been right when she'd said Sultan had given her a notebook for her flowers? Impossible!

Maria and I stopped outside and waited until Jannat was finished yelling at Stella. We heard the broom swish across the bare courtyard, and then a pile of broken glass was swept outside the front door. Jannat's head appeared at the bottom of the doorway, as if she were squatting on the floor.

I pulled Maria behind the open door, but not soon enough. Jannat caught the movement of Maria's bright pink dopatta and lashed out at us. "And where did you die? You're never home. Always following Tara, as if you're her tail."

Maria started mumbling before she made eye contact with her mother. "We saw a *munyari wala* selling all kinds of cloth and red glass bangles near the canal. You would have liked what he was selling. I thought I would come and tell you."

Maria's lies sounded so true, even I wanted to believe them. Falsehoods became the truths she told her mother to protect herself from being beaten. Lies were her self-preservation. They were how she made sense of life.

"What would you tell me? That your father has found gold in the gutters. That I could exchange that gold for a new outfit and the scarlet glass bangles. What was written for me is worse than I thought. Stella can't walk. You walk and talk too much. My babies are dead. What am I left with?"

"Don't say that, Amman," Stella said from her perch on the *peerhi* in the courtyard. "God blesses us all with his brilliance."

Stoic Stella had spoken. If her sister's chattiness grated my nerves, Stella's level-headedness destroyed them. What made her so calm in such chaos? Jannat felt as I did.

Jannat's glare couldn't penetrate her daughter's calm, so she used words instead. "God must have blinded me, then, because I see nothing. He didn't choose you or me to bless."

Jannat brushed the last pieces of glass to the left of the doorstep. They sparkled in the sunlight. She stood up, and her knees made a noisy clicking sound. She threw the broom in the corner and, without looking at Maria, addressed her.

"Collect the pieces of glass, Maria, and add them to the pile of glass in the bin. When the garbageman comes along, we can sell the glass, but don't let him trick you by giving you cane-sugar crispies in exchange. Take cash."

Maria looked away, as if in protest. The money from broken glass was never worth much, and the crispies were such a treat. Jannat pretended not to notice and continued her tirade. "Well, who else will give us money? Tara's bespoken mother, Bibi Saffiya, doesn't care for us. She just keeps piling on more work for me, without ever paying me. You know what she said last week?"

Maria and I stood silently. We knew she didn't care for our answer. My thoughts wandered to the previous week, when I had found a crumpled five-rupee note under Bibi Saffiya's bed as I was straightening the covers. It was tied tight in the corner of my dopatta. Maria knew about it, but it seemed she'd either forgotten or wasn't betraying my secret for the time being.

"That's enough, Amman," Stella said softly.

"Enough for whom? You don't even want me to tell the truth. You're all liars, and when I tell the truth, you tell me to be silent."

"We know the truth, Amman," Stella persisted calmly. "We

know that we're of another faith. We know that we're poor. And we know we must work for the rest of our lives. What else is there to know?"

"Nothing. There's nothing to know. Go! Both of you. All three of you. Maria, hold your sister's hand so she doesn't stumble. Take her to her corner in the big house. And keep that hero Sultan away from her. I've seen how he stares at her. Your father will kill him before I can get my hands on him."

Stella's face turned orange as she looked down, embarrassed by her mother's crassness.

I twisted the *chameli* garland on my wrist, now wilting in the heat of the early morning. I wondered if Maria would tell her how Sultan had pinned it to my braid that morning. A few buds fell on the newly swept floor, and Stella looked at them. Was she thinking of pressing them in the notebook Sultan had given her?

The thought upset me. I felt self-conscious and awkward. To build my confidence, I started rambling, saying the first thing that came to me: "Jannat *khala*, Bibi Saffiya will expect you to be early today."

"What's the problem now? What's happening today? I come early every day. Why should I come earlier? I washed the courtyard yesterday, and now my back is killing me. She thinks we're animals. We don't need to rest."

And then I remembered the conversation with Bhaggan from the previous night.

"Amman Bhaggan said you might get paid today. She was paid yesterday, so she's going to the shrine to give a *deg* of biryani, large enough to feed all the supplicants, a gift to the pir to pray for Sultan *bhai* to pass his eighth-grade exams."

Sultan's name triggered another mouthful from Jannat.

"That son of an owl. He'll never pass his exams. She thinks

he'll save her from that hell of a kitchen. But her kismet is no better than mine. At least she lives in the house and doesn't have to pay the electricity bill. I have a hundred expenses, and we all work, but nothing to my name. Tell Bhaggan I want to go, too. I have some prayers that have not yet been answered."

As I thought of the money I had taken from under Saffiya's bed, I wondered what I would buy. Maybe a bottle of shampoo or a soap to entice Sultan away from Stella.

As if she had read my thoughts, Stella caught my eye and I looked at her cloth bag, covered with practice embroidery stitches that she'd done using leftover multicolored threads.

I had checked that bag once when she had gone to the bathroom. Inside was a red rag with five different-size needles pinned to it. One plastic pouch was filled with skeins of silk threads, and another one was filled with thicker cotton threads. Two small pairs of scissors were wrapped in a rubber band and had been slid into a side pocket. None of this had interested me then.

"Here, let me take the bag," I demanded. I wanted to see if Maria was right about the notebook she said Sultan had given her sister. I ran to pick it up and glanced inside when I did. The bag held more than embroidery materials. A heavier object weighed it down, and as I placed it on my shoulder, my fingers traced the straight lines of a cardboard-covered book at the bottom of the bag. I caressed it and then rushed ahead, not wanting to hold Stella's hand as Maria helped her sister stumble toward the house.

Wild Boar and Snakes

The time of necessity is nearly on us! What took you so long?" Amman Bhaggan wanted to know.

"Massi Zakia fainted, and we had to stay till she recovered." This was a half-truth, but I was proud that it was not an outright lie.

Amman Bhaggan rolled her eyes, then opened her mouth wide, revealing her half-rotten teeth. She let out a long, drawn-out yawn, followed by a tirade about not having had enough sleep the previous night, first because of the storm and then because of her fear of the boars.

"They forgot to put castor oil outside the door last night, and I couldn't sleep. The cat was crying—so ominous. Maybe it smelt the boar. And then this morning the kittens were gone. Good riddance, I would say. Maalik would have to throw them in the canal, like he did last time, when we couldn't care for them."

Every night, Amman Bhaggan reminded her sons to pour castor oil near the courtyard doorway to keep the boar from breaking down the door, should they smell the goat waiting to be slaughtered on Eid day. Her tired eyes were more troubled than usual.

"I shut my eyes for a few seconds, and the dead visited me,

so I hurriedly recited a prayer to keep them at peace. You never know when an evil spirit will cast a spell on what we hold dear."

She knew firsthand the danger of boar coming too close to humans. "One year, when my uncle returned from the fields after cutting the cane, he was chased by a boar." She repeated the story as if to forget what was troubling her. "The vile boar ran by Hajjan's house. It stopped when it saw her sitting, preparing meat for the meal the next day. It could smell the fresh goat meat and decided to join her."

I didn't remember having heard this gruesome story before. I wasn't sure why it had just come to her.

"It ate the meat and then took a bite of her," she continued. "That's how she lost her left foot."

Bhaggan gestured to me to take the wooden comb from her hands, and then shut her eyes, anticipating my running the softened bristles through her henna-dyed hair, and continued the story.

"Years later, at her son's wedding, Hajjan could barely carry the pitcher with his ceremonial bathwater, and she limped down the street. Everyone danced around her to the wedding drumbeat. Instead of singing praises of his garlanded rupee notes and his floral headdress, she swore at my uncle. But it wasn't his fault. He didn't know why the boar had followed him."

There was always a prevention or a remedy for such a calamity.

"Castor oil distracts wild boar. It smells of their own fat. I've seen them turn right round if they get even a whiff of it."

I'd seen Amman Bhaggan pass the castor oil bottle to her sons and then rub the oil from her palms on her scalp. It kept her alert, she said.

She also vowed that her hair, her pride, stayed strong and beautiful because of the oil. Granted, the thick, dark mane now had a streak of an orange cascade from the henna she used to cool her scalp in the summers. Now a veillike scalp cover, it had been integral to her few years of married bliss.

My combing had relaxed her. The twist in the story reflected her mood.

"I had a thick braid and small feet, and that's why Sultan's father married me. He didn't see me before we were married, but when his mother came to see me from the village close by, it didn't take her long to convince him that I was the catch of our village."

I'd heard this story, like all the others, about her light eyes, how her future mother-in-law thought they might be a bad omen, but when her husband-to-be looked into them on the day they were married, he said they were the color of Himalayan acacia honey.

"He said I had trapped him," Bhaggan recounted, her eyes still shut, as if she needed to calm herself. "Little did I know that his entrapment would be for such a short time."

A rasp of sorrow caught at her voice. "My husband would serenade me at night, singing, 'Oh, lover with light eyes, I will stay with you forever.'"

Bhaggan sat quietly with her eyes closed, but the romance she memorialized was short-lived. She didn't have to repeat what had happened next. I kept combing her hair.

He didn't stay with her forever. Forever for him was two years.

The day he left, never to return, Amman Bhaggan placed two rotis covered with desi ghee in a red cotton cloth, along with a piece of his favorite gum-berry pickle, for him to eat in the fields.

But this is where her love story took a horrendous turn. Tears welled up every time she told us about it. She took the corner of her dopatta and wiped her face.

"I waited for him that night. Three days later, they brought back his body, bloated by the canal waters. It had been caught in the reeds and scared the women washing their clothes. Their screams reached the village, and Lal Mohammad, the snake charmer, came to see what had happened. Lal saw the snake wound around my man's hand and went immediately to the canal's edge to urge it out of hiding."

But, as if it knew what was in store for it, the snake remained hidden.

So Bhaggan and her mother-in-law both wailed over his body. They tore the dopattas off their heads and screamed to the heavens to avenge their sorrow—one for a young son and the other for her lover. Bhaggan broke her glass bangles and began her *iddat*, the required days of seclusion after her husband's death to ensure she was not pregnant.

It was difficult to imagine Amman Bhaggan as a young woman in love. I shut my eyes and thought back into her memory.

In the one-room hut, they had been ardent lovers and she had indeed conceived their third child the night before he left on his last journey.

I imagined how it would have been in that time before morning, as the last stars lit the night and the maulvi prepared himself for the morning prayers.

I re-created a memory that she had never described, but it was lovely nonetheless, and I imagined it could have been true.

He would have turned around and looked at his sleeping wife, and she, when she awoke, would have looked directly at him. Her acacia honey–colored eyes would have lit up their corner of the room. In quick silence, they would have fulfilled their passions, and then, wrapped in each other's arms, fallen asleep again.

The next morning, she would have known that they had made another baby but would have to wait a month to confirm it. The confirmation came only after her husband's death. And as she sat in *iddat*, the four lunar months and ten days of required mourning for her husband, she realized she would be bearing this child of extreme love and great sorrow. Maalik, the youngest.

Salt in the Millstone

Unlike the maulvi and Bibi Saffiya, Amman Bhaggan did not pursue peace in the five daily prayers. She searched for it in the courtyard of the shrine of Sain Makhianwala, where she returned in times of necessity, in times of sorrow, and in times of joy, which penetrated her life as often as a fly finding its way through the mesh food cover and Bibi Saffiya's swatter.

That morning, while I combed her hair, she told me of her dreams for her two other sons, which were dependent on Sultan's success. He worked hard, she reminded me, as the wooden comb scratched a scab behind her ear. She wiped away the drop of blood with her dopatta, not letting it deter her from completing her vision. Sultan would pass his exams and get a job as a teacher or a policeman in the city, and he would take them all with him. We didn't know anyone who had those jobs, but I joined her imagined life of comfort in the city.

All three lives depended on Sultan's triumph in school. Maybe Bhaggan knew what I knew: that the struggle in class was a burden for him. That the salt crushed at the millstone had it easier than her son, straining to read and write under the lamplight. She must have thought that voicing her hopes as reality would give them strength to flourish.

Her visits to the shrine filled the void that her dead husband had left. The shrine replaced the one who had promised her a life of comfort and love. She told me of some of her visits, and others I imagined. She told me about the crowds, the aromatic smells of street food, and the communal kitchen, but what fascinated me most was the toys she described: cloth dolls; brightly colored trucks and buses, like the ones on the road; toy horses and cattle; and tiny kitchen utensils. I felt my face relax into a smile as I thought of how much I would enjoy such treats.

"Daughter, do you see any lice?" Bhaggan distracted me from my daydream.

"The itch has been driving me crazy. It might just be prickly heat." She sighed. I parted her hair to check and told her that it was clear—no lice, no prickly heat spots—but that didn't pull her out of her despondency.

As I pulled at her hair to braid it, she told me about a time before Maalik, her youngest, was born. Bhaggan went to the shrine of Sain Makhianwala to give an offering of a chicken because Sultan had been scorched with fever for three nights. He complained that he couldn't eat because his throat was scratchy.

Not knowing what to do, she asked her mother-in-law, whose own five children had died before they could celebrate their first Eid. Bhaggan's husband, the only surviving child, was taken to the shrine every year to ward off evil. His mother's efforts to give him a long life included letting a section of his hair grow longer than the rest. She dressed him in girls' clothes and even got him a silver ankle bracelet. And it worked. He lived longer than the rest.

Bhaggan shared her mother-in-law's suspicions about why the baby Sultan would not recover.

"It's an evil eye on my son's laughing, playing household, I'm telling you. Amman Hajjan, the witch, left small bundles of paper with black magic. She's done it before, and now she wants my whole family to perish."

Like her late mother-in-law, Bhaggan was desperate to know the reason for her family's ill fortune, but she knew it wasn't the old hag Amman Hajjan, who sold candy, tobacco, and trinkets from the corner of her room outside her son's home. Why would she try to kill her customers?

Bhaggan chose not to take a chance with her baby, Sultan, and went to the shrine early on a Thursday, a day when prayers became pronounced, more likely to be heard. As with any other problem, Baby Sultan's fever would be reduced by an offering at the shrine. She told me how she had bought four rupees' worth of sugar balls and threw them energetically on the shrine and then watched the beggars scramble to pick them up.

She also took a white chicken and had it slaughtered and cooked at the communal kitchen, for more blessings to be bestowed on her sick son. The sugar balls reinforced the strength of the chicken meat and created balance that would stabilize her life. Having accomplished all this in one morning, Bhaggan went home to continue her work in the kitchen.

She had cooked the meal earlier and returned to bake roti in the tandoor. She remembered the event from eleven years ago as if it were yesterday. Her anger toward her mistress was also aroused with the same intensity as she had felt back then.

"Do you know what Saffiya said?" She did not wait for me to respond; Saffiya's words were engraved in her mind. "She said, 'Where were you, Bhaggan? I waited for my massage before my bath, but you never came. People usually say when they're not coming.'"

Bhaggan ranted about how offended she was. About how

first her man had been bitten by a snake, and then her baby, Sultan, not even three, shaking with fever and a sore throat, and how her *beeji*, her dead man's mother, said she should go to the shrine to pay her respects and present a chicken. And that the only one she could afford was a farm-raised one, instead of a desi one. A desi one, she told Saffiya, would have more power for her poor Sultan. Saffiya should have understood all this. She knew Taaj, her second son, was still being breastfed when another baby had begun to grow inside her. Her name was Bhaggan, the blessed one, but her life was cursed to the core.

Bhaggan's anger at Saffiya from so long ago had not receded. It boiled over to that morning as I combed her hair.

"I told her, and, like a nervous cat, she scratched at a pole. You know what she said?" Bhaggan continued, and, again, I didn't have to answer. "She said I should have told her. She would have sent me to the hakim in the city. She told me to give her her meal and have some faith in the higher powers. She would send me to the hakim who was her father's friend— may his soul rest in peace, and may he be sent to the highest levels of heaven. There was no one else like him around here. I don't know how he had such a daughter like Saffiya. Despite being such a great landlord, he went out of his way to help all the poor people in the village."

I don't know if Amman Bhaggan told me about this, but I could imagine Bibi Saffiya grunting as she reached under her pillow for her green cloth wallet.

"Here, take ten rupees and take the baby in the tonga tomorrow morning. My father's friend the hakim will give you some powerful medication to cure the baby immediately. Just go after my massage, because you know I can't really do anything all day if I miss it."

Saffiya would have then lain back on the charpoy that she rarely left, and Bhaggan would have automatically started to massage Saffiya before her mistress began to complain about her aches and pains.

"My back is killing me, and my digestion is also terrible. The gas has gone into my muscles and is causing me great pain. I'll go to the hakim, too, but once the car has been serviced. I still need to find some time to go."

Bhaggan would have taken the ten-rupee note and tied it in the corner of her dopatta. But before she could leave, Saffiya would have reminded her to prepare the next meal. "And, Bhaggan, bring some tea for me at five o'clock. Warm the milk on gas, not on the dung fire."

Bhaggan's anger toward Saffiya didn't last long. Her devotion to Saffiya mystified me. She never questioned their relationship long enough to leave her.

But that was all so long ago. Before I came, or maybe it wasn't. Maybe it was my imagination.

For her firstborn, Sultan, the one I had tried to entice with a *chameli* garland that morning, Amman Bhaggan had many dreams. The dream of the moment was to see him pass his eighth-grade exams. And she would do everything in her means to accomplish this, even if it meant feeding the beggars at the shrine of Sain Makhianwala.

The morning after Maria and I returned from Jannat's house to help Stella to her usual embroidery spot in the rooms inside, after I had combed her hair, Amman Bhaggan reminded me.

"My daughter, Tara. I'm going to the shrine this afternoon," she told me. "Can you finish your work and not get into trouble?"

"Me?"

"I see the garland on your wrist. I'm just surprised that she didn't." For all that Bhaggan noticed, I couldn't understand why she chose to ignore what was sometimes so pronounced, like Sultan's incompetence, Taaj's nastiness, Maalik's stupidity, and, most of all, Saffiya's meanness.

"Everyone is always after me. What have I ever done?" I responded.

"Nothing. You never do anything. It's just your attitude."

"What about my attitude?"

"Swallow your anger. Finish all your work, and I'll get you the doll I promised. When I go to the shrine."

I didn't think I wanted a doll anymore, maybe some earrings instead, but if I changed my mind, Bhaggan would act suspicious. "Why earrings and not a doll?" she'd ask, and I wouldn't have an answer.

"And for me, too!" Maria called from outside.

I wanted to go to the shrine with Bhaggan to look at the glass bangles and beaded necklaces I had seen when I had gone. Then, Maria and I had wanted the dolls that were now ragged, and if I went, Maria would want to go too.

I knew Amman Bhaggan would not take both of us. She took Sultan instead. He had to carry the *deg* of biryani on his head. It had cooled down a bit before he asked his brother to place it on the rolled cloth stabilizer perched on his skull.

"Come, Taaj, help your brother carry the *deg* on his head," Bhaggan called.

"He's the eldest and the strongest. Why can't he do it himself?" Taaj whined.

"Son of a dog. Why do you make me curse my dead husband? Come, and don't make me waste my breath."

I decided I would show how mature I had become, so I stood in front of Sultan, with the *deg* between us, and looked intensely at him, willing him to make eye contact. Taaj came and stood next to me, brushing against me.

I stared at Sultan and bent over. I realized that my neckline was now visible, since I had pulled my dopatta tightly around my neck, so it no longer covered the area that it was supposed to protect.

I looked up at Sultan and knew he had been staring at my breasts. I pretended to pull my dopatta closer, but as I did, I elbowed Taaj.

"It's nearly time for the afternoon prayers." Amman Bhaggan beckoned as she slipped on her slippers and left the kitchen.

When she left, Taaj moved closer and brushed his arm against my breast. I nearly dropped my side of the *deg*. Sultan kept it balanced and saved it from slipping, we heaved the pot onto his head, and he followed his mother to the bus stand.

No longer feeling as mature as I had felt earlier, I kicked Taaj as he followed his brother.

Maalik and Taaj would walk up to the cane fields. They would both break themselves off a piece of cane to chew. They would stand near the canal close to the house and spit out the chewed-up sugarcane, devoid of all the sugar they would have sucked out. They would then see how far downstream the chewed cane husks would flow before disintegrating.

Neither Maria nor I was allowed to go that far, so I shouted as they left, "Bring me a cane, too, brothers."

The Shrine of Sain Makhianwala

❧

Sain Makhianwala, the patron saint of the shrine, the Keeper of Flies, the man who had lain for a hundred years in a grave covered with red, green, and gold satin shrouds, had never taken a bath.

I had seen men like that on the roadside. They stayed away from the village. They had no use for family or home or food like the rest of us. Amman Bhaggan said God had given them the power to stay alive, and that when he took them, their graves marked a special place for forgiveness and blessings.

Sain Makhianwala had come to the village at a time when there were no buses or cars or electricity. He had come to remind the villagers, the farmworkers, and their families to cherish all life, even flies that contaminated food and carried sickness.

"He sat motionless for hours, letting flies and maggots live off the filth on his body. Cleansing himself would kill a living being," Amman Bhaggan told me. "Dogs would lick the salt from his sweaty body. That brought him closer to God," she added.

"Such a holy man!" She sighed. "Everyone goes to his shrine, and he blesses sinners and saints alike. When I took Jannat to pray for sons, she got two. She couldn't care for them, but that was on her. Bibi Saffiya herself went before her wedding. Her prayers were answered: She returned to the village within a year. Sain Makhianwala doesn't discriminate. And everyone believes in his powers."

Not everyone, I thought.

Even before I had visited the shrine, Amman Bhaggan's veneration of Sain Makhianwala's bodily filth had intrigued me. To amuse myself and the others at morning religion lessons with Zakia, the maulvi's wife, I mentioned the holiness of the Keeper of Flies.

As if the fumes of Sain Makhianwala's unwashed body had emanated from the shrine, spread across the cane fields, and engulfed Zakia, she breathed heavily and then began her tirade on how even a dead body needs to be washed before it's placed in the ground.

I wondered if that was what had happened to the holy man —if he had spent his whole life distancing himself from water, only to be bathed once he was dead.

Zakia must have rambled on in anger about the torturous consequences of flouting the rituals of religion, cleanliness being key, but I was no longer interested in what she thought. I did, however, provide an opportunity for the others to stop memorizing the lines they had been repeating for the past ten minutes.

Visions of hellfire reflected in Maalik's dilating pupils as he listened to Zakia's decree. Taaj, as if to tempt fate, drew unmentionable body parts on the ground with his finger, daringly close to Zakia's line of sight, though she never turned her head in his direction. Perhaps he knew she wouldn't.

The two sisters, Hamida and Nafissa, fingers stuck to the words on the page of the Qaida, rocked soundlessly, hypnotized by what they heard.

I turned my gaze toward the maulvi, wondering what he thought as he sat silently, listening to his wife, smoking his hookah. I caught his eye, but he looked away and gestured to Taaj to bring a fresh coal from the stove, where Zakia sat overseeing the preparation of the day's meal.

The lesson stretched to eternity as Zakia's wrath persisted.

But when we returned to Amman Bhaggan's kitchen, I asked if the maulvi had ever gone to the shrine to ask for mercy for being married to such a woman. She laughed and said I would get myself in trouble for such thoughts and promised to take me the next time she went to the shrine.

Amman Bhaggan kept her promise and took me twice after that.

The first time we went with an Eid offering. Bibi Saffiya had sacrificed one black and one white goat that year. The white one was for all the luck she needed for herself, the black one in memory of her father, dead for more than a decade.

Amman Bhaggan distributed a third of the meat among the villagers and kept another third at home.

After consulting with Bibi Saffiya, she took the leftover meat to the shrine, ensuring continued blessings for the crops and cattle for the next year.

Remembering her promise, she said, "Bibi, the two girls, Tara and Maria, want to go, too. I'll take them for an hour and return before the afternoon prayer."

"They'll just be a nuisance. They can stay behind. I'm sure there's plenty to do," Bibi Saffiya grouched.

Maria and I stood behind the door of Bibi Saffiya's room and held hands tightly, as if this would give Bhaggan more power to convince her mistress to take us.

"We have two pots, and you know my knees. I'll have to get them to help me load and unload."

We heard Bibi Saffiya clicking her tongue disapprovingly. We waited for her to suggest that Taaj or Maalik, Bhaggan's sons, help with the task, but she didn't.

Maria squeezed my hand, and I stopped biting my lip as I heard Saffiya ask Bhaggan to pass her the keys to her cupboard. I could hear her shuffling to the cupboard door and opening the heavy lock.

"Here, take the bus fare for the four of you, but don't forget to return the change. And tell the girls not to make a habit of wanting an outing so often."

Gulping down my anger at Saffiya's suggestion that a yearly outing was one too many, I let go of Maria's hand and straightened my clothes, excited for this first trip to the shrine that I had heard so much about.

The next morning, after breakfast, we would take the bus and leave the meat with the cooks of the shrine. They would prepare a meal to distribute among the supplicants. With full stomachs, the beggars and holy men would have more power in their prayers.

The power of prayer might help even me. What would I pray for? My true mother? A family? A home?

I'm sure I didn't sleep that night. I had to think of the perfect prayer so that Sain Makhianwala would hear it at the shrine. Amman Bhaggan had explained that to be heard, I had to be respectful in my prayer. First an invocation to God, and then a *durood* to the Prophet. Only then should I think of myself.

If I asked for a mother, would that make me happy? I wasn't sure. What if she were like Jannat? Did I want a mother like her? If I asked for a family, I might be happier. A home with a family would be even better. I would keep all my options open. I would make a list, say it quickly, and then wait for the most deserving prayer to be acknowledged.

I was up before the rest the next morning. After breakfast, Amman Bhaggan and Sultan carried the pots of meat on their heads, and Maria and I walked behind them on the canal banks through the cane fields.

Maria trailed behind and twice dropped her two rupees, the money we had received for Eid from Bibi Saffiya. The second time she dropped the money, I helped her tie it in her dopatta, like I had done.

When we reached the main road, I grasped Maria's hand, sensing her terror among the overcrowded, whizzing buses, trucks, vans, and bullock carts. Men were holding on to the backs and sides of the vehicles, and some were even sitting on top, holding the side rails to avoid toppling off.

The vehicles were all decorated with paintings of birds and beautiful women. Dusty silk scarves in pink, blue, and green fluttered from the tiny mirrors on each side. Even the bullocks were dyed bright pink, with jewel-like bells proclaiming their arrival.

Maria pulled her hand away from mine as she pointed at a man dressed in women's clothes, with his face covered in pink and white makeup. She looked up at me and smiled, but I made a stern face, not knowing how else to respond.

I stepped back to avoid the sparks and ashes of a cigarette flying out of a bus. Two men holding hands sauntered by, and then a crowd of passengers exiting from a bus on the opposite side of the road crossed to our side.

"Give me your hand," I told Maria. Sultan had told me of the pickpockets at the bus stop, but I was worried Maria might get swept away in the crowd.

Buses flew by, not stopping, a layer of dust settling on our group as they disappeared into the horizon.

After a while, Amman Bhaggan asked me to help her take

the pot of meat down from her head, and I struggled. She would rest while we waited. I was not used to traveling on a bus, and I wasn't sure how we would make them stop. Sultan kept stretching out his right hand while steadying the meat pot with his left. The brightly painted buses rushed past, choosing to ignore we meat carriers.

Will we ever get to the shrine? I thought, brushing a fly from my nose. It landed on Maria, who tried to squat on the dusty roadside, but I pulled her up. Amman Bhaggan had already made a seat of her meat pot. Then, as I glanced toward the cane field from which we had walked from the village, I saw a familiar figure walking toward us. Dressed in flowing white garments with a red-and-white-checkered shoulder cloth, the maulvi appeared as our savior.

Maria let go of her money knot to wave at him and then excitedly turned to Bhaggan to announce the maulvi's arrival.

Amman Bhaggan stayed seated but looked relieved. We all had our reasons to get to the shrine as soon as possible, but time was not cooperating. Surely, the maulvi could help.

"*Bhai* maulvi, you're like rain on a hot day. I have to return before the afternoon prayer, and the bus drivers have all sworn not to take anyone from our village to the shrine!" she called to him, before he was within hearing distance.

He came closer and said, "I'm going to the shrine. Let's move to the next corner, near the tea stall, and we should be able to catch a bus."

He was right. A slightly tilted bus swerved toward us and stopped long enough for us to struggle on. First, Maulvi climbed up onto the bus, turned, and took the meat pot from Bhaggan and pushed it toward the back seat. Then, taking her hand, he pulled her up and shoved her toward the pot. I scrambled up after her and pulled up Maria. Sultan placed his pot on the step, and I dragged it up in time for Sultan to jump onto the step.

We had not yet found our way to the back seat when the driver hit the gas and we stumbled onto the passengers around us.

"Bastard. Son of an owl!" Amman Bhaggan shouted at the bus driver, as she pushed the meat pots under the seat.

Maria and I sat on either side of Bhaggan with the meat pots beneath us while Maulvi and Sultan held on to the pole in front of us, swaying with the moving vehicle.

After an hour of churning in the bus, we stiffly descended to the dusty path to the shrine. The maulvi told Bhaggan that there was still an hour until the afternoon prayer. I wondered who would call for prayer back at the village, considering he had chosen to come to the shrine instead, but didn't want to offend him by asking.

He led us to the shrine, creating a path for the meat carriers. As we left the bus stop, we were surrounded by peddlers enticing us with guavas sprayed with lemon and chilies and baskets overflowing with glass bangles. I pulled Maria past these distractions, reminding her of our original plan to buy a pair of dolls so we could arrange their marriage and celebrate it by inviting Hamida and Nafissa to sing wedding songs.

We struggled through the path that the maulvi, Bhaggan, and Sultan had created for us. I thought of the dresses I would tell Maria to make for the bride's dowry. We would ask Hamida's mother, who sewed clothes for all the village women, to give us the leftover material that she saved for patchwork quilts. I had seen a whole bundle under her charpoy.

Maria would buy the bride doll and I the groom. Then, after they were married, I would get both. I would let Maria take her doll home when I chose, because I would be the mother-in-law, with more power. After all, I would have the male doll.

The thickened crowds indicated that we were approaching the entrance to the shrine. Now the peddler carts were filled with shiny flags and satin shrouds for offerings to the Keeper of Flies. Some of the shrouds were printed with holy words, like the ones we had learned with Zakia, and others had gold embroidery.

Bhaggan told me how supplicants could buy the shrouds as offerings to cover the grave of Sain Makhianwala. They would layer them on over the previous shrouds to make their prayers more prominent than those of the previous petitioners.

I had seen the layered shrouds at the graveyard near our village. The holy man buried there was not as miraculous as Sain Makhianwala, but some of the villagers believed that he listened to their prayers. The less fortunate villagers tied prayer rags on the tree covering that lonely little grave, but I had never seen crowds like I was witnessing at this shrine. All of them wanted their prayers to be heard by the great saint. And he heard them all—the people, and the flies that hovered around them.

Flies, the true worshippers of their protector, covered the carts selling sugar balls, bright candies, fruits, and toys.

I pulled Maria toward a pair of cloth dolls on the cart farthest from us. It was the perfect pair, a bride and a groom made in grayed-out white cotton. Their identical, large, staring black eyes were kohled with thread, the tiny red lips permanently sewn into smiles of joy.

A red-and-gold wedding dress covered the bride, and tiny ear and nose rings were sewn on forever. The groom's face was hidden behind a veil of shiny tinsel, and on his head was the most perfect wedding turban.

I picked up the groom, opened my money knot, and handed my two rupees to the man standing next to the cart. Maria hungrily grabbed the bride and did the same, but she couldn't find the money knot on any of the corners on her dopatta. She let out a wail.

Maulvi, who had followed us, placed his hand on Maria's head and asked her why she was so sad.

"My two rupees Eidi are gone," she whined.

Maulvi dug his fist into his side pocket and pulled out some coins to pay for the doll, but before he handed it over, Amman Bhaggan puffed from behind us, "They can play with one doll."

"I can't stand seeing little girls cry," he responded as he paid the salesman on the other side of the cart. The man counted the money carefully, and stuck it into a pocket sewn onto the front of his vest.

Maria and I held our dolls tight and followed the adults, now entering the half-open gate to the shrine courtyard. The smells and sounds overwhelmed me. I covered my nose with my dopatta, disguising my confusion with the demeanor of someone who visited the shrine often.

The shrine itself was not as large as I had imagined. Mosque-like, it had an onion dome, but instead of walls, doors, and windows, arched pillars supported the roof. In the center of the shrine, the grave of the Keeper of Flies was elevated and covered in layers of shiny prayer clothes.

I squinted to focus on the bright green satin sheet covering a mound barely visible behind the columns. The crowds of men surrounding the grave of Sain Makhianwala held their hands high in prayer. Even though the building was slightly smaller than the village mosque, the men standing in it far outnumbered the number of villagers who entered the mosque.

I wanted to push past the crowds to move closer to the grave, so my prayers would be heard, but Maulvi held me back.

"No, my daughter," he said. "Women are not allowed inside the building. Stay here and pray. You will be heard."

Bhaggan and Sultan placed their meat pots on the floor, and we all stood with our hands held high and prayed as hard as we could. I also wasn't sure how I would get a family and a home with just one prayer. But I prayed anyway.

We didn't linger. We handed our meat offering to the cooks, whose outdoor cooking area was on one side of the shrine, and returned soon after, excited about our new pairing of dolls that we would spend many hours marrying and divorcing. We were so engrossed in the pleasure of our new toys that the journey home seemed uneventful.

THE SECOND VISIT to the shrine came a year later. Amman Bhaggan had been unwell for a few months. None of Bibi Saffiya's herbal remedies had any impact. She had even gone to a local dispensary to get energy pills, but she continued to burn with fever. Her breathing was unsteady, and her whole body ached. I spent hours massaging her, but nothing seemed to work.

She decided to go to the shrine for a night of prayer as a last resort, and since she was delirious and unsteady, she took me with her.

This time, I was more confident. I knew where to stand for the bus and stretched out my hand aggressively for it to stop. I held Amman Bhaggan's hand as she stepped into the bus, and I even pushed one of the men standing near our seat, who kept falling on me when the bus swerved.

We arrived after the sun had set and the evening prayer

time was almost over. I pushed our way to the shrine entrance and found a clearing for us to sit and rest.

I remembered that the maulvi had cautioned me last time about how women and girls were not allowed to enter the building, for fear of impurities that they might bring with them, so we stood near the archway facing the grave and prayed.

My prayers were slower this time. They were the same as before—a home, a family, and, if I were very lucky, a loving mother—but I knew it would take a long time for all those prayers to be heard.

Amman Bhaggan had a lot more to ask. She started by mumbling prayers for her dead parents and then for her dead husband. The blessings on the dead would strengthen the prayers for her health.

She started with a mumble, and then tears rolled down her pockmarked cheeks. I couldn't help but start crying myself. Her pleas became more frantic and louder. She wanted to see her dead mother again in her glory in paradise. She wanted all her own sins to be washed away and all her miseries to be drowned. She wanted Bibi Saffiya to return the money that her husband had given her as a down payment for a lot of land. She wanted her sons to be as faithful and true to her as her husband had been. She wanted sons for her sons so they could continue the family lineage for years to come. She wanted each son to have one wife, or two, if he chose, and for the wife or wives to be caring and loving to her grandchildren, as she had been to her sons.

At the climax, she prayed that she would die with her sons and grandsons around her, so they could all lift her body, wrapped in the white death sheet, and take her to her next life, so she could transcend and join her parents in paradise.

I was weeping uncontrollably with her, and, exhausted, we sat in silence for some time. After a while, I could smell the evening meal being cooked in the same outdoor kitchens where we had left the meat we had brought during our previous visit. The aroma of freshly baked roti comforted me in these unfamiliar surroundings. A wealthy landowner must have had a good crop that year, or maybe he had found a second wife or given birth to another son, and the supplicants at the shrine were benefiting from the offerings.

I left Bhaggan and returned with a stainless-steel plate of steaming chicken and two rotis. I ate hungrily, but Bhaggan's appetite still had not returned, so we threw the leftovers to the dogs that sat staring at us from a distance.

We sat in contented silence when the drumbeats began. First one, then another holy man, a fakir, stood up to dance in frenzied circles around the drums. I had not noticed them earlier that evening, but, one after another, men with long, gaudily patched, tattered green shirts and unruly, tangled hair began twirling to the drumbeat.

The tempo increased, and a female fakir joined the others. Her hair, like theirs, was an uncombed mess, unwashed and matted. She inched toward the center of the dancing men, circling faster and faster, leaving the drumbeat behind, controlling the others with a dizzying force.

The spinning dervish hypnotized us all. I looked away to gain some control. But Amman Bhaggan chose to drown herself in the circling frenzy. Her eyes had whitened, like those of the fakirs. She stood up, and her feet began to move in time to the drumbeat.

"Allah hoo, Allah hoo," she repeated.

I wasn't sure if I should join in or stay seated. I decided to stay where I sat. The frenzy both scared and fascinated me. I'm not sure how long it lasted. The drumbeat, the chant, the feet, the dance, the heat. We were all hypnotized.

The female fakir continued to lead the dancers as they now circled the drummers, who dropped their heads but continued the beat in a trance.

And then, one by one, the dancers collapsed in small heaps of silence. The flies that had been aroused by the vibrating sound and movement settled in mounds on the fallen dancers, obscuring them.

Dolls' Wedding

Taaj and Malik never returned with the cane from the cane field that afternoon, so Maria and I decided to marry our dolls under the *shahtoot* trees while we waited for the others to return and the sun to recede.

Most of our afternoon activities were innocent childhood explorations that the adults frowned upon, so we waited until obligatory naps during the hottest time of the day silenced the house. Then we danced among the trees like movie heroines or ate mouthwatering sour, unripe mangoes or loquats from the surrounding orchards, secure that Saffiya and Bhaggan would never know.

Sometimes Taaj and Maalik joined us, but other times, Maria and I placed a charpoy in the shade of the *shahtoot* tree to catch the intermittent warm breezes as we played with our dolls. We made make-believe homes and make-believe schoolrooms. Worlds parallel to our reality. Worlds the way we wanted them.

That afternoon, Maria and I prepared for our dolls' wedding by mixing henna in a bowl and making dotted designs on our hands to cool ourselves off. We hummed wedding songs and sat the two limp dolls on the charpoy next to us.

Before Bhaggan returned, we decided to play the part of the wedding that the village women joked about—the part that no one ever saw, after the wedding guests had all left and the bride and the groom were alone. Bhaggan would have words to say if she ever found out. She would probably even beat us with slippers. But I didn't care.

Maria spoke up, surprising me with her knowledge: "Amman makes moaning sounds at night when she lies next to my father."

"How would you know? You sleep with me." As always, I questioned her credibility.

"Remember the time Amman Bhaggan was unwell and you spent the whole night tending to her? Amman Bhaggan told me to sleep at home with Stella that night."

How could I have forgotten? I had been afraid that Bhaggan would not live through the night and that I would be left alone.

"Stella told me to keep my head under the blanket because it was so cold. But it wasn't really cold. And then I farted." She looked at me and laughed.

I continued, straightening the bride doll's clothes, covering her face with her tinseled scarlet dopatta. The groom doll's face was covered with four grimy strings of gold thread. I folded the cloth dolls, seating them close together, and then propped them up with rolled fabric.

"Well, do you want to know what happened?"

I didn't want to appear too eager, so I remained silent at Maria's question.

"Only if you want to." Maria knew she had caught my attention, so she continued.

"Amman and Abba were sleeping on the charpoy in the other corner of the room. I could hear Amman making strange noises. Abba was on top of her, like this."

Most villagers had two-room homes, one for sleeping and

the other for visitors. Jannat and Isaac had a one-room mud house, with three charpoys on each wall.

Other villagers piled the tin storage boxes in their second room and covered them with crochet and embroidered clothes. None of Stella's embroidered clothes ever found their way to her parents' home, so the boxes filled with clothes donated by Saffiya, which included some old sweaters and a threadbare gray coat, hid under the charpoys in embarrassment. And on one wall, a chipped blue-and-white vase and a framed picture of a woman with a tiny baby sat on a shelf.

Taking the groom doll from his perch, Maria placed him on top of the bride doll, toppling them both. With her other hand, she covered her mouth, stifling a giggle. I frowned for her benefit, and for any grown-ups who might have seen us. I didn't know if she was telling the truth, but I sensed this was not just her imagination.

Taaj had once thrown a rock at two stray village dogs, and they had yelped away. When I'd asked him why he had done that, he'd laughed and said they were doing what men and women did in bed. I hadn't believed him, and he'd wanted to tell me more, but Amman Bhaggan had called me away.

I didn't want to believe Maria knew more about this than I did.

Dried brown henna crumbled from Maria's hands onto her doll's blood-red bridal outfit made of scraps of shiny materials from Bibi Saffiya's sewing basket. I couldn't stop staring at the dolls.

"Nothing will happen if you keep looking!" Maria was enjoying her supremacy, so I decided to build up my confidence and respond as if I knew what we were talking about. I knew babies came after a wedding, and I knew if it was a boy, the celebrations would be greater than those for a girl. I knew when a man got too close to a woman, a baby appeared sometime after.

"If the dolls have a baby, it's mine," I said.

"You'll have to wait for the baby." Maria took pleasure in knowing more than I did about such matters.

"Not me," I declared. Nothing I was saying made much sense, but I wasn't going to let Maria have the upper hand. Whatever I did, I would keep my ignorance hidden. I knew women were responsible for bearing children. Wasn't that what Zakia complained about to Saffiya and Bhaggan?

The dolls lay in a pile of crumpled roses and marigolds that we had plucked to decorate their marriage bed. Between the crushed rose petals and the marigolds were sprinkles of henna. I pulled the yellow petals from a marigold and chewed on the bud. Maria did the same with the rose. We looked at each other, not sure what to do next.

I wasn't having fun anymore and needed to pee, but was too lazy to go to the fields, so I ordered Maria to look away.

I pulled down my *shalwar* and relieved myself on the parched ground near the tree.

Maria wrinkled her nose. "Oof, Tara."

"What did you expect? That's how it smells."

"What?"

"When a baby is made." I was tired of Maria's knowing all the answers. And for now, I added, "It's how your mother smells." Bhaggan had mentioned that Jannat smelled of urine, even though I wasn't sure why.

"That's because she's unwell," Maria said.

"No, it's because she keeps having babies."

"Not my mother. Your mother . . ." She stopped short. Maria was a better person than I. She knew when she was being hurtful and apologized immediately. "That's not what I meant."

I pretended to be offended by the reference to my nonexistent mother. Everyone knew I didn't have one. Maria had heard it from Bhaggan many times, and also from Saffiya. Bibi Saffiya told the story of how she had found me. Her version was not the same as Bhaggan's. In her version, Saffiya seemed more saintly.

"It must have been divine intervention," Saffiya was fond of saying. "I had just finished my afternoon prayers and was saying the salaam at the end, when I looked to the right and then the left, and saw the bundle of clothes on the seat opposite. It had been left by the young woman who got off the train immediately after I began my prayers. She was covered from head to toe in a burka. She looked like a town girl. Her burka, you know, it was decorated in the fashion of town folk. Overdone, if you ask me. Not like us village folk, who keep our wealth hidden."

My mother had been a woman of consequence. Otherwise, why would she have been on a train and wearing an embellished burka? Not a village woman, not like the rest.

"I thought she had gotten off the train to get something to eat, but when the train started to move, I realized the woman wasn't planning to return. I looked out the window, but she was nowhere to be seen. Then the bundle moved. No one else in the train. Just me and Bhaggan. It was as if I were getting a sign from above."

Was I a sign from God? Was that why I was special?

"But the train had already started moving, and when Bhaggan picked up the cloth, she saw this little rascal. I named her Tara, Star. Did you know I named Jannat's daughter Stella? Their names have the same meaning. You know how names can make the future? How else would they both be able to anticipate a bright future?"

Was this true? I thought. If Stella and I had the same name, would our destinies also be the same?

"Tara didn't cry. I don't think I've ever seen her cry. She was like that the day we found her," Saffiya ended.

"Never cried," Amman Bhaggan chimed in. "Someone would have sat on her, and she wouldn't have made a sound."

I took pride in having never cried in front of anyone. Even when my mother had left me on the train. My scowl and laughter were renowned, but I had never cried in front of anyone, and no one would ever make me.

Maria had belittled the mother I had never known, but I would never cry.

"Of course you had a mother before they found you." Maria was now embarrassed and spoke nonsense.

But I would not forgive her easily. My response, about her beginnings, would reflect my pain. I looked directly at her and spoke calmly, adjusting Bhaggan's version of Maria's birth to reveal how I felt about her now.

"I was there when you came out of your mother. She screamed and I watched as I sat in the window. And they stuffed her dopatta in her mouth. And then Hamida's mother told her to shut up or she would wake the whole village. But everyone was already waiting in the courtyard. Waiting to see if she would have a boy or another girl. It was just before the early-morning prayer, and they thought they were waiting for a boy, but then you came and they started beating their breasts like Shia on the tenth of Muharram. You were small and dark and ugly. And they hoped you would die. But Amman Bhaggan came in and hid you away under her bed. And she kept you hidden for a whole year, until you were too big to die!"

Maria looked back at me, tears streaming down her grubby cheeks.

"You're lying," she cried. "You always tell lies. Amman told me not to play with you. She said you're the devil. You do magic and cast the evil eye on everyone."

"Get lost! I never asked for your doll. You wanted to marry her to mine." I kicked the copulating dolls onto the dampened patch I had just created. I covered my head with my dopatta and ran past Maria.

The Cane Fields

〜ℒℒℒ〜

The dolls' wedding was a disaster, but the afternoon was nearly over. This time, Bhaggan believed her offering at the shrine would ensure Sultan's success. The previous two times, he had failed his exams because of the evil eye. One of the village women might have been envious of Sultan's accomplishments, and so they had cast a spell causing him to fail. She should have gone to the shrine earlier, instead of burning red chilies on the open fire to ward off the evil eye.

The effort was tiring, but the reward would be great. Mother and son returned victorious, confident that blessings had accompanied them home.

"My beautiful daughter, bring me some water before I faint."

Maria and I trailed after Amman Bhaggan, looking expectantly at the bundle she carried under her left arm. She used her dopatta to wipe the sweat from the back of her neck, then stumbled and lurched in search of her space on the *peerhi* in the kitchen.

Maria showed her concern in the best way she could, by rubbing Bhaggan's feet, while I ran to get her some water.

"They're swollen like loaves of bread," she said, as she

pulled off Bhaggan's slippers and wiped the dust off her feet with her dopatta.

I cleaned the steel glass with my dopatta as I squatted in front of the pitcher. It took me a couple of tries before I could fill the glass with the tepid water. Some spilled on the floor as I tipped the pitcher toward me.

"Careful—you'll have to fill the pitcher with sweet water if you keep watering the kitchen floor like that." Bhaggan's exhaustion didn't stop her from chastising me. "And get a lump of ice from the freezer, but make sure you fill up the trays to make ice cubes for Bibi Saffiya before dinnertime."

I returned with the water and massaged her back while Maria rubbed her feet, and she continued.

"If this trip doesn't save my life, it will kill me, but Sain Makhianwala heard my request. I asked for your Sultan *bhai* to pass his exams and then become an officer in the government and get a good salary to pay for the house that his father was going to buy. You know, the one my husband gave Saffiya the down payment for."

She gulped the water and then chewed on the ice and blessed us both.

"May you find a husband as good as mine. But may he have a much longer life. You are better than daughters I might have had."

Bhaggan's wishes flew over the head of Maria, who looked up from her perch below as she shifted herself to a comfortable squat. "But what about the dolls, Amman?"

Playing at dolls' weddings seemed like a waste of time now. I wished Maria would grow up.

Before she could answer, I made a suggestion that would appeal to Bhaggan and show her how grown-up I was, compared with Maria.

"Shall I make some tea for you first? There's some leftover milk in the fridge, and it still has the cream on top."

I didn't wait for her to respond. I ran toward the fridge in the indoor kitchen. I had softened her edge.

"*Bus, beta.* That's enough." Amman Bhaggan indicated that Maria should stop now.

"Pass me my *potli*, and I will open it up and give them to you." Maria passed the *potli* to her so she could get her hands on her doll.

It didn't take me long to make the tea, but I had to rush to pull it off the fire before it all boiled over. As I sucked my nearly charred finger, Bibi Saffiya's high-pitched voice called out from the inside rooms. "Are you back?"

"What does she think?" Bhaggan muttered. I knew she had no patience for attending and listening to her now.

"Amman, you sit and I'll go tell her." I felt good being in control. I looked at the dolls in Maria's lap. They were both female dolls. We wouldn't be able to play our marriage game anymore. I wished I had asked for some glass bangles instead. Even some earrings, now that Amman Bhaggan had pierced my ears a month earlier. It had hurt, but now that the swelling had reduced, I could replace the soiled green thread with some dangling rings, if I had any.

I would let Maria take both dolls.

I straightened my dopatta and ran to Saffiya's room to see what she wanted.

It was time for the afternoon prayer, and she needed her tea and rusk. The aroma of the sweetened, smoky, milky tea boiling over onto the fire must have slid into the inner sanctum of the house and awakened her from her afternoon nap.

I prepared and brought the tea tray to her room, but as I poured the cup, Amman Bhaggan yelped from the kitchen, distracting me, and the milk spilled on the already soiled floral tablecloth. Bibi Saffiya and I looked at each other, and she rolled her eyes.

"Tara, my daughter!" Bhaggan called again.

"Go listen to what she has to say, and then come back to take the dishes when I'm done," said Bibi Saffiya.

I covered my head and pulled down my sleeve to hide the *chamelis* on my wrist, now wilting in the late-afternoon heat.

"And bring the flyswatter when you return. I've told you so many times to leave it near my bed," Bibi Saffiya reminded me.

Amman Bhaggan sat filling the servants' cups with the dark, dung smoke–flavored, raw cane–sweetened tea.

A fly buzzed around her, and she blew twice to get it out of the stream of the boiling liquid, but the third time it flew directly into the stream, struggled a bit, and then, as if giving in to a sweet death, whirlpooled into the scalding, milky tea. Bhaggan pinched it out and threw it to the corner of the kitchen. This mesmerized me until she brought me back.

Her call didn't seem as urgent now.

"Go, my daughter. Sultan has left his notebook in the kitchen. He has to study for his exam with his tutor this evening, and I've already made him late. He shouldn't have gone far."

"It's been so long since he left," I said, feigning reluctance. But in fact I was ecstatic for the opportunity to see him without an audience. I'd straighten the *chamelis* on my wrist, now darkening with the heat.

"Run, my *jaan,* and you'll catch him before he reaches the main road."

Taaj, who had joined his mother for tea, looked up at me with a knowing smile.

"I would send Taaj, but he has to help Maalik feed the buffalo before evening," she explained. "I'll clear Bibi Saffiya's tea dishes while you're gone."

"Be careful of the wild boar in the cane field," Taaj whispered, as he sipped his tea.

"What nonsense!" Bhaggan threw the kitchen cloth at him, and a few drops of tea fell on the notebook.

"It's all wet now," I protested. "What will Sultan *bhai* say when he sees it?"

"What will he say? He'll be glad that his mother has thought of him."

Bhaggan's euphoria seemed to be slipping into despair again. "Tea stains are nothing compared with how my life has been marked. My husband left and never returned. I was left to care for my children and my mother-in-law, and since then I have served Bibi Saffiya. A wet note-book is nothing compared to what I have endured . . ."

I slammed the kitchen door as I left, not wanting to hear the rest of the story or see the smirk on Taaj's face.

I passed the kitchen window sedately and then picked up speed as soon as I left the vicinity of the house. I rushed past the village and the one-room mosque, crossed over the stream, and then made my way to the first dust road, hoping to reach the pathway that would take me to the main road, where Sultan would be walking to the next village. A retired schoolteacher there prepared the village boys for their exams. He must not have been that good, considering how many times Sultan had attempted them. Maybe he should find another teacher.

The pathway led me past the cane fields. I wished Taaj had not made that comment, but I had only heard of the wild boar. I had never seen them.

I rushed past, more to avoid the distaste of seeing one of

the village elders relieving himself. The only reason the boar would have left the nest at this time would have been to bring back sustenance for their young. Motionless cane fields were safe. Rustling cane might seem like the result of a warm breeze, but there was usually a wild boar; at least, that was what I had heard. I held the notebook close to my chest and rushed on, trying not to breathe, to avoid being noticed by anyone or anything.

Once the fields were behind me, my fears were alleviated. I loosened my grasp around the notebook, but I realized it was a little like holding Sultan's hand, so I tightened it again.

I remembered how that morning he had been silent when his brothers had made fun of his marrying me. Had his silence meant agreement? Maybe. Had he enjoyed wrapping my braid with the garland of *chameli* now wilting on my wrist?

The light breeze gave me confidence. Good weather meant great fortune.

As I jumped over the canal, my foot slipped on the muddy bank and I fell forward. I looked around, embarrassed that it would reduce the grace I tried so hard to project, but there was no one around, so I didn't worry. I brushed the front of my *kameez* and stood up.

Finally, I could see him in the distance. Alone, as always. I might have called to him to stop him from going farther, but I decided it was too vulgar to do that. Only the village women would call out across fields. Bibi Saffiya would wait until she was closer, and I would do the same. Even the heroines in the TV dramas I had seen were poised and aloof.

I struggled to wipe the mud off my slippers on the grass, and as I did so, I nearly lost my balance and the notebook fell. When I picked it up, a few loose pages slipped out. I wished I had learned to read, but, as much as I tried to put the words together, nothing made sense. I flipped through the pages until I got to the last one.

A pressed rose, exactly like the ones I had seen in Stella's embroidery design book, taunted me. Stella must have given him a token of her love from her collection of pressed flowers.

I let the rose drop into the mud and then, with my already muddy slipper, pushed it deeper. I wished I had crumpled it before I had dropped it, to destroy it completely.

How had I let this happen? Why would Sultan prefer Stella, the illiterate, limping girl who sat in a corner embroidering flowers on pillowcases? Had I made a fool of myself flirting with him that morning?

My feet no longer felt the need to rush. I took a few more seconds to wipe all the mud off my shoes. I watched Sultan's figure get smaller and smaller, and I no longer cared. And when he reached the main road, I decided to return. I walked past the cane fields again, not caring about the villagers relieving themselves, not caring if a wild boar came out and pulled me into those deep, dark, sugary rows. I heard a rustling, but it was just a field mouse sucking on the side of a cane that someone had cut and decided wasn't sweet enough to take with them.

I passed by the mosque and looked in to see if anyone was in there. The door was locked, but the window was open. I could have climbed in, like Maria and I had done many times before, but I chose not to. I no longer had the urge to enter where I was not supposed to go.

The notebook was still with me. Now it had mud, as well as tea marks, on its cover, but at least it no longer held within it the ugly pressed rose.

The Wail

stared in horror at Sultan's oiled hair. It was still combed as if nothing had happened. His body, covered in a white shroud, stretched on the charpoy that he used to share with his brother. Without thinking, I reached up to the now-shriv-eled *chameli* garland barely hanging on my wrist. The flowers were no longer white. They had aged within the day. Why had I not destroyed them as soon as I'd gotten home?

It was time for the evening prayer. The wailing in the courtyard had drowned out the maulvi's voice from the mosque.

It hadn't taken us long to gather around the charpoy in the middle of the courtyard. Four villagers, followed by two po-licemen, had carried the rope cot in, holding on to the crudely carved poles.

I had finished washing the tea dishes, and Amman Bhaggan had been preparing the evening meal. Now she stood at the foot of the charpoy, tearing out her hair and looking to the skies.

"My beautiful boy! You would have passed your exams. You would have become the groom every girl wanted to marry. You would have had sons, as many as you wanted. As beautiful as you. As intelligent as you."

"That's enough, Bhaggan. Find peace. God takes from us

the best of what we have." Bibi Saffiya spoke from the charpoy that was placed at a safe distance from the body on the charpoy covered in flies.

The white shroud was soaked with blood. Flies buzzed all over it. Amman Bhaggan now sat at the foot of the charpoy, one hand covering her head with her dopatta, the other fanning the dead body of her favorite child.

"I did it to him. I praised him and cast an evil eye on him. I should not have praised him, and then others would not have been so envious of him," she mourned.

I looked around the courtyard. The police van had brought the broken body, which looked as if it had been run over by a bus, squashed in the center. Two officers stood in the corner, drinking glasses of warm water. It had been hot that afternoon. But now it seemed even warmer.

Why had he been run over by a bus? Was I to blame? If I had brought him the notebook, would that have delayed when he crossed the road?

I looked across the courtyard at Stella. Had my jealousy caused his death? Was it because I didn't want her to have him? But I didn't even like him. I didn't like the smell of eggs. I couldn't remember it now. I had already forgotten the smell of his coconut oil.

I looked away from Stella. I could not bear to see the pain on her face. She sat staring at the bloodied body in the middle of the courtyard. She stared at Bhaggan and the wailers. She held Maria's hand tightly. Then she tugged at it, and Maria looked down at her. The sisters communicated without saying anything, and Maria helped her sister to walk toward the body.

I approached Amman Bhaggan in silence to try to rub her feet, but she wouldn't let me touch her.

As her screams became louder, more village women joined

the mourning wails. I didn't recognize some of them. They had come from the village across the canal. They had heard the sirens and now the wailing. I didn't know that they had known Sultan. I had never seen them in Bhaggan's kitchen. They were here to help her mourn.

One wailed, "You left your mother all by herself. You self-ish son. How could you have chosen to go before her? How could you have chosen to be with your maker before it was your turn?"

Another joined in, "You were always impatient. You were always wanting more than your share. And now you have taken it. You wanted to be with your father. You chose to be with him, rather than stay here with us."

Another slapped her own head with both hands. "What a beautiful prince. There will be no other like you." As she wailed, the woman pulled Maalik and Taaj into the circle and said, "Pull your hair, tear your clothes. Why do you continue to live? Why do you not join your brother?"

The two boys looked at their mother, not knowing how to respond. I wasn't sure either. When Bhaggan had talked about death, it had been about old people, or people who were evil, who needed to die. Sultan had been neither.

I watched as Stella took the fan from Bhaggan's hand and sat on the other side of the body. Slowly, she started fanning his head, and the flies flew away from his face. Then she took her dopatta and wiped the blood off his cheek.

She sat there until the maulvi told the women to leave so he could cleanse the body and prepare it for burial.

I felt weak. I couldn't stand. I hid in our room. It was dark and hot, but I didn't care. I waited until it was dark outside.

No one would cook in the kitchen today. The house of death was also the house of starvation.

TIME OF NECESSITY

Sanctified

○◦◦◦○

Three years had passed since the morning when I had enticed Sultan to pin the *chameli* garland on my braid, the day that had ended so tragically with his death. His death changed our lives in ways we had not anticipated.

Bhaggan still went to the shrine, but her prayers were not of hope, but rather of solace in her despair—a sorrow that she hugged close, as if releasing it would make her plunge into an abyss. She would not recover from the loss of Sultan.

No longer did she participate in the annual festivities by distributing sacrificial meat at the Eid celebrating the pilgrimage, or by cooking semolina pudding for Eid breakfast after the month of fasting. Bibi Saffiya asked Hamida's mother to come and help me until, by the third year, I was able to manage it all myself.

Bhaggan continued with the daily cooking, but I had to remind her to peel the potatoes or add salt to the lentils, until I took over those chores, too. She stopped bathing regularly and wore white to remind us that she was still mourning her beloved son.

The day Sultan died, Bhaggan sat all night at the foot of her dead son's charpoy. His body lay covered with a blood-stained white sheet. Stella sat near his head and fanned the flies away from the white sheet covering his oiled hair.

The next morning, the maulvi washed the scarred body and covered it in a clean white shroud to bury it in an unmarked grave next to his father.

I envied the stamina of Stella and Bhaggan, so dedicated, so loving. I needed to do something to memorialize him, to show I could love like them. The *chameli* garland was brown and wilted, but it was the only tangible evidence I had of our connection, so, like Stella, I decided to save my memory by pressing the garland in a book.

I chose the purple brocade–covered Holy Book Amman Bhaggan had gifted me, recited the prayers for forgiveness, and closed it on my memory of Sultan with the flowers. Over the years, I'd opened the book and the flowers on occasion, but each time, that prompted the petals to keep disintegrating, until only a few brown, odorless remnants of my first love were left.

Sultan's death changed us all.

In the three years afterward, Maalik, the youngest, became his mother's dependable son. He didn't say much, but he joined Bhaggan when she had to travel to the shrine. He stopped attending lessons with Zakia and decided to leave school. The only time I heard him speak up was in response to Saffiya when she called him in to admonish him for not appreciating her support in paying his school fees.

"I can do more for myself and my mother if I work in the fields, rather than waste my time with books," he'd say. From then on, Maalik took on the role that his brother Sultan had vacated in death.

Taaj, the second son, disappeared after Sultan's burial. He ran away. And then, for the next three years, he continued to run away, only to return when he needed food or funds. He'd hitch rides on buses from the main road. Jumping on as they sped by, risking his life, tempting fate, as if in hopes of joining his brother.

On each return, Bhaggan would spoil him by cooking his favorite food, in an attempt to keep him at home and out of trouble, but with each departure he became bolder in the risks he took.

Maria talked less. She no longer asked questions. She smiled less. She spent less time with me and more with her mother.

Stella stayed in bed after the burial, and none of Bibi Saffiya's remedies could make her return to her daily routine of embroidering pillowcases in her designated corner. She was so listless that we all thought she might die of heartache, until one day Bibi Saffiya decided to take her to the hospital in the city.

Saffiya called for the village taxi because there was no way that Stella would have been able to walk to the bus stop. Maria and I carried her to the taxi and laid her on the back seat. I sat with her head in my lap, and Maria placed Stella's feet on hers. Bibi Saffiya sat in the front seat, next to the taxi driver. This was the first time Maria or I had ever sat in a car, but by now we didn't share our excitement about such novelties.

An hour later, we reached the hospital, which was run by doctors and nurses of the same faith as Stella. They wore long white robes and covered their heads, but not with dopattas. Some had fair skin and spoke the same language we did, but it sounded different. Others looked just like us but wore the same dress as the others.

Maria and I waited in the hallway while Saffiya took Stella inside. We sat quietly for a long time, stunned by the misery of the patients around us, who had come with their own families.

In one corner stood a huge glass box. Inside was a tall man dressed in flowing robes, but he was not made of cloth. He was like a huge doll. He stood with both hands raised and tendrils of hair on his face. He looked kind. He reminded me a bit of the maulvi, but he was much younger.

"That's the savior, Eesah," said Maria.

I didn't care that she knew something I didn't, so I didn't acknowledge what she'd said. Now that she'd said it out loud, I knew who this was—Christ, the Christian God.

When Saffiya returned, she was alone.

"They will take care of her," she said.

We returned home that afternoon, without Stella.

SIX MONTHS LATER. Maria and I joined Saffiya to pick Stella up from the hospital. There she stood in the same hall with the huge statue of the savior in a glass box. Saffiya left the three of us outside and went in to talk to the doctor.

"Christ is not a man. He is God. He loves all and is loved by all," Stella told us, and then she crossed herself quickly in a prayer for the beloved. Maria's hand brushed mine questioningly, but the words stayed captive inside us.

Stella pulled a small bottle of rosewater from her pocket and sprinkled it on the glass box, a tradition she had learned when she had attended holy recitals at Bibi Saffiya's house. Maybe our religions were not that different, as Zakia had always taught us. I mumbled a memorized prayer.

The aroma of rosewater and strong *chameli* attar was the scent of purity, perfection, paradise. "Just like Sultan," Stella said, facing the statue.

I wasn't sure whether it was the smell or the statue that

she was referring to, but I thought I understood. She had a special bond with Sultan, which I had never felt. The stale coconut oil and sweat engulfed my thoughts, and I looked at Maria. She returned my gaze but chose not to engage longer.

I followed her line of sight to the statue in the glass box, which stared lovingly at the three of us. We stood in a warp of silence as a fly whizzed past us, mesmerizing us with its frenzied flight. As if intentionally, the fly found its way into the glass box through a small opening of broken glass. The statue, unfazed by the intrusion, continued to stare lovingly at Stella.

I knew that Stella would never forget Sultan. I knew, as she stared at the statue of Christ in the glass box, that she was really thinking about Sultan, replacing in her mind's eye Christ's long, flowing brown hair with the darkened, oiled hair of the only man she had loved.

Stella told us she had started to learn how to read fluently. She had also begun a journey of deep devotion.

She hugged her sister, Maria, and then turned to me and held my hand in both of hers. I looked at my feet, my mind clear of thought. She hugged me, too, and, without asking for assistance, limped away from us.

Earrings with Pomegranate Seeds

It had been nearly three years since Sultan's death, and the boys and I had also stopped going to Zakia's house for lessons. No one called me in to reprimand me about this decision.

I was relieved not to see Zakia on a daily basis. Only at village events, like Eid, or a death, or sometimes a wedding, would I encounter her, but I took pleasure in not acknowledging her presence.

"Don't, my daughter," Bhaggan reprimanded me, after I'd left the kitchen one day as Zakia had entered to visit her. "She's not a happy woman, but it's not her fault." Bhaggan had softened since her son's death.

"Why do you even talk to her?" Bhaggan had betrayed me with this simple act. "What did she want from you, anyway?" I added.

"What have I left to give? She wants me to put in a good word to Hamida's parents on behalf of her nephew. He's a schoolteacher, but he's not very smart. Hamida's parents want to know why his first wife left him. How can anyone know what happens between two adults behind closed doors?"

"The one who was at Hamida's cousin's wedding, sitting outside near the buffalo? He didn't have the sense to sit with the other men under the marriage tent," I said, now curious whether Hamida's parents would agree.

"Maybe, but I don't think they'll give their daughter to him. Zakia wants the maulvi to convince them, but he's not getting involved," Bhaggan responded.

The maulvi must have known something about the schoolteacher that the others didn't. I knew he would never agree to something his heart was against. I sought out his blessings when we met by bowing my head close enough for him to pat it in acknowledgment with a prayer.

"You're growing tall, my daughter. Are you taking care of Amman Bhaggan?" he would say.

"I wasn't always going to stay small" was my usual cheeky response.

Over the past three years, I had taken care of Bhaggan like any good daughter. But I was no longer the little girl who had made *chameli* garlands to pin in her hair before going to study the Holy Book with Zakia.

I was taller, but my body had also grown in other ways. My breasts moved when I walked, so Bibi Saffiya gave me an old bra, which I tightened. I wore it every day and sometimes even at night.

The first time I wore it, I could tell that everyone was looking directly at my breasts, so I wrapped my dopatta tightly around me to avoid the embarrassing stares that stole all my confidence. But once I gained confidence in the control of those straps, I enjoyed the attention.

Every morning, before Taaj and Maalik left their charpoys in front of our room, I took a quick bath with the blue plastic bucket that I filled at the water pump. Sometimes I wore the same clothes I had slept in, but I always braided my thick, oily hair with a black cotton *paranda*, lengthening the braid and making it swing seductively around my buttocks as I returned to my room.

I never looked back at them, lost in a half sleep, but I could sense their desire as I sauntered toward the outdoor kitchen where I prepared parathas and tea for their breakfast. After breakfast, I took on more work in the kitchen. I learned how to cook the meals for the day. And in the afternoons, I took care of Saffiya's personal grooming, braiding her hair and massaging her body when it grew tired of the tedium of sitting on a charpoy, talking to the villagers in an effort to address their personal and financial disputes.

Bhaggan had given up all of these lighter duties before Sultan had died. For me, these were opportunities to daydream in the comparative silence and cleanliness of Saffiya's room.

Regularly, I trimmed Saffiya's nails with a blunt clipper and rubbed her heels with a terra cotta pumice stone in the afternoons, but in the evenings I would perch myself on the bed and massage her back and legs and watch soap operas on TV. Saffiya would drift in and out of sleep, and I would lose myself in the intricate lives of characters that seemed so real.

Now that three years had passed since Sultan's death, Bhaggan had started to participate in some of the Eid celebrations. She still didn't bathe or wear new clothes for the event, but she took her seat in the center of the kitchen to oversee all the meals.

Saffiya had bought three goats to slaughter to celebrate the Eid of sacrifice, the black one for her father, the white one for herself, and the speckled for her husband. Bhaggan oversaw the slaughter, and I distributed the plates of meat among the villagers.

The crop the previous year had allowed Saffiya to purchase a deep freezer, so we made packets of the rest of the prime pieces and stored them away for as many months as the freezer would allow. The whole ordeal took two days.

By the third day after Eid, exhausted from organizing the meat with Bhaggan, Saffiya sat on her charpoy on the veranda with her feet dangling over the edge. I sat at her feet, rubbing olive oil into them to soften them. As I pulled her left foot toward me, I looked up at her. "Bibi, I've heard there's a new cream that makes your skin white and softens it till it glows. The TV ad goes, 'Black skin becomes fair, and fair skin will shine like the moon.'" I mimicked the singsong jingle.

"You watch too much TV," Saffiya responded lazily, placing her right foot in front of me so it got the same treatment as the left.

Then, after a pause, she added sharply, "Get lost, idiot—the lemons from our tree lighten my skin, and the olive oil from our olive trees makes it soft. You haven't wasted your Eid money on the cream, have you?"

For Eid, I'd received five rupees from Saffiya and two from Bhaggan, who, even though she no longer participated in the celebrations, gave all of us two rupees as a celebratory gift.

I was saving my money. I wanted to buy earrings. Maybe ones of real gold, like the ones I had seen on the heroine in the movie on TV. The heroines in the soap operas were always more servile and never seemed to have enough to dress well, until the day they were married, and then they were covered in shiny clothes and layers of jewelry.

I preferred the heroines of the movies. Like they did, I would wear earrings, dress nicely, and go to the movie theater.

Taaj had told me about the movie theater one of the times he had returned from his escapades. Maalik thought it was a waste of money, but it sounded so glamorous—a gigantic building with a huge screen and people bigger than real life.

"It was as if I was sitting next to them on the hillside while they sang songs and danced in the rain," Taaj said, laughing. "I would take you. We would see the new movie *Love and Honor*," he told me, though he seemed to say it in jest. I sat peeling the garlic pods, and when I looked up, Maalik was waiting for my response to his brother.

"You'd have to dress nicely, though," Taaj added. "Wear nice clothes and earrings and glass bangles, and we'd sit in the box. Only men sit in the seats down below. Women sit with their men in the boxes so that other men don't bother them."

"Who said you're my man?" I pretended to be upset by his insinuation, but it enveloped me in a warmth that I had not anticipated.

"We can slip out in the afternoon when everyone is sleeping and return before the evening prayer," Taaj responded. All the while, his younger brother's censorious gaze preventing me from agreeing.

I felt the warmth return as I sat rubbing the olive oil into Bibi Saffiya's feet and hoped I had not given my thoughts away.

"When you're finished with my feet, make me a nice cup of tea," Saffiya's voice intruded.

To ensure that I was not a wastrel, I responded to her previous comment, "No, Bibi. I never waste my money. And anyway, I got only two rupees from Amman Bhaggan. What can I buy with that?"

Saffiya's nostrils, swollen with dust allergies, restricted her ability to smell the penetrating rose scent of the cream Taaj had already gifted me. Even if she could have smelled it, she was too preoccupied.

She wiped the mucus from her nose with her dopatta, cleared her throat, turned her face away from me, and spat. Then, looking directly at me, she announced, "Zakia is coming next week to propose for her nephew the schoolteacher, and I'm going to say yes because you have no reason to disagree. She said you were eyeing him at the wedding in the village."

A marriage proposal should have made me happy. I had always wanted a family of my own. But the nephew was not young, and Hamida's parents must have already turned Zakia down when she had asked for Hamida's hand. If Hamida's parents had done that, why did Bibi Saffiya think I would marry him?

"What?" Saffiya's mood was exposed through her bulging eyes.

I stared at the green sputum on the floor and continued rubbing her foot, the oil dripping on my favorite yellow *kameez*, creating a stain that would remain until it would be torn into dusting rags.

My thighs were now weak and trembling from squatting for an hour at Saffiya's feet. She sprawled above me on the charpoy and adjusted the circular embroidered cushion behind her back. The cushion reminded me of Stella. Saffiya talked down to me.

"I'll talk to Bhaggan. She'll remind you of what is good for you. That's enough, now. After tea, get my dirty clothes from the bathroom and wash them carefully, but hang them in the shade. You ruined my blue outfit. The sunlight bleached the color out of it. I'll have to dye it again."

I stood up with unstable legs, surprised that I was not as angry as I should have been. I felt calm. I knew what I would do.

On Eid day, Saffiya had placed her traditional earrings, *jhumkas*, with rubies like pomegranate seeds and tiny white pearls, in a white cotton packet under the Holy Book covered in red satin. She'd looked around and then closed the cupboard door. From the bathroom, I had seen her hiding the earrings.

I'd busied myself before Saffiya noticed that I had seen where she had hidden them.

My legs still shaking, but now for other reasons, I entered Saffiya's bedroom and straightened the bedcover, even though no one had sat on the charpoy since I had changed the bed-sheets that morning; then, as I walked toward the bathroom to collect the sheets and Saffiya's dirty clothes, I snapped open the padlock on the almirah that I had left unfastened, despite Saffiya's having ordered me to secure it that same morning after I had made the bed. Sliding my hand into the cupboard, I pulled out the small cloth packet with Saffiya's earrings from the top shelf under the red satin–covered Holy Book.

Securing the padlock without making a sound, I walked into the bathroom and stuffed the earring packet into my bra. Sweeping up the soiled bedsheets and Saffiya's clothes from the damp bathroom floor, I walked briskly to the water pump to wash them.

There were times when I respected Saffiya like a mother—not my own, who had deserted me on a train, but like mothers in movies and on TV. I felt a twinge of affection for Saffiya when she gave me one of her old outfits to adjust to my size, or an extra piece of leftover dessert that she shouldn't have eaten anyway because of her rising blood sugar.

But arranging my marriage with Zakia's nephew? I thought she knew me better than that. Instead of a mere schoolteacher with no land to his name, she would have chosen someone with more standing, not a reject. A mother on TV or in the movies would never do that!

Betrayal

⤙⤙⤙⤙⤙

I sat at the hand pump in the late afternoon and washed Saffiya's clothes. I spread her green *shalwar kameez* on the charpoy in the shadow of the *shahtoot* tree. It lay there as if it were her flattened, dead body. Any feeling of loyalty or love I'd had for her had dissipated that day. Anger pushed against my insides, emanating through my entire body. My pounding heart deafened me.

How dare Zakia say I was interested in her demented nephew? And had she been spying on me? Marrying Zakia's nephew was out of the question. If Hamida's parents had decided that he was not good enough for her, I, the adopted daughter of Saffiya, had a lot more to offer than the lowly daughter of a farmhand.

As I raised my arms to spread the rest of the garments on the clothesline, the gold earrings hidden inside my bra scratched my breast and gave me pleasure. I wouldn't let anyone—anyone—get away with treating me this way, even if it was my own benefactor. This would not be the only way Saffiya would have to pay. I would show her that I might not have parents to back me, but I knew how to take care of myself. Even now, if I opened my eyes wide enough, I could stop my tears from flowing. I would save them for the night. I would not make a spectacle of myself.

I returned after washing the clothes, but Saffiya continued with her tirade. The prayer break had not pacified her. Her abuse was at its zenith.

"So, a schoolteacher is not good enough for you? A princess without a palace. You have a good reason for turning down a perfectly good proposal?"

My anger contested hers with silence, making me reckless. I wanted to shout back at Saffiya. I wanted to tell her that I was far from a princess, as was evident by how I lived, and that I knew the proposal of Zakia's nephew wasn't what I desired. I clenched my hands and felt a throbbing deep in my head. I knew she was still talking, but I'd stopped. I stared at her, narrowing my eyes to contain the tears of anger that hung like dewdrops on the *chameli* leaves, evaporating in the morning sun. I had stopped breathing and began to feel light-headed, but contained myself to avoid a deep breath that Saffiya might interpret as the weakness of a sigh.

Soon I let her insults slide over my freshly oiled, *chameli*-scented braid, neatly tucked into the black *paranda* I had bought with Saffiya's money that she hadn't given me. A week earlier, I had found three five-rupee notes under her pillow as I'd made her bed. I had swiped them cleanly from the pillow as she'd sat facing the window. Any guilt I might have felt now washed away in this tirade of my not accepting the proposal of the weasellike schoolteaching nephew of my archrival, Zakia.

Zakia needed to know her place, which was not to decide my destiny. I had stood up to Zakia for Hamida when we took lessons from her. Granted, we didn't continue meeting much after that, but I had heard that Hamida had not improved her reading or her cooking abilities since then.

And Saffiya—she might have taken me in as a baby, but that didn't mean she owned me.

As if to answer my thoughts, she yelled, "I've spent all my life caring for others. Y-y-you bastard, you've never been grateful! Remember, I saved you. I gave you a roof over your head and a bed to sleep on. Others would die for a sheltered life like yours."

Unable to stand still while her abuse continued, I took the corner of my dopatta and started to wipe the dressing-table mirror. In the reflection, I could see her folding the prayer rug and placing the rosary next to it in preparation for the evening prayer.

I then picked up the silver kohl bottle and rubbed it hard, as if the intricately designed kohl stick would magically silence my tormentor, but she continued. "You're an uncaring idiot. Mark my words, I will keep the dowry I've been collecting: the bedsheets, the pillowcases that Stella embroidered before she left, everything—I will keep it."

I placed the kohl bottle noiselessly on the glass shelf on the dressing table. Then I began to pull Saffiya's graying hairs from the pink plastic hairbrush. I made a small ball of the hair and placed it in the trash can next to the dressing table. I did not look up.

"Did you hear what I said, Tara *bibi*?" Sarcasm dripped from her mouth like baby drool.

My shoulders stiffened, and I sat anchored to the ground, like the cow that stiffens when she realizes she's the one chosen for the Eid slaughter. The celebrated one. The one that will end her life to benefit others. The gift that is cubed and stacked, with blood seeping through the muslin that keeps off the flies.

I knew my silence infuriated her, and the inside of me smiled.

I looked into the mirror again as I mechanically screwed the lid back onto the brown, rusting olive oil can. Then I stood up, straightened my *kameez* with one hand, and walked calmly toward the closet to return the olive oil to its place on the second shelf, behind the talcum powder with the picture of a half-dressed woman with an alluring gaze. I picked up the powder and tightened the perforated top, and a cloud of dust rose toward me and then sprinkled onto the cement floor, creating a slippery patch that I wiped with the back of my slipper, spreading it further.

On any other day, this act would have maddened Saffiya and she would have told me to bring a damp cloth to wipe away the patch of powder, but this was not one of those days. She was still stupefied by the pressure of my silence. I stood with my back to her.

I fiddled with the lock on the cupboard, remembering how Taaj had wooed me over the past few months. How he had brought a small bottle of shampoo for me. How he held my hand when he gave me the basket filled with vegetables from the village, or the time he pulled my *paranda* to get my attention, pretending it was an accident.

Taaj was very different from his brother Sultan. Had I been deluded by my attraction to the elder brother? Was it really the outgoing and adventurous Taaj whom I would have preferred?

I imagined how he'd keep his promise and take me to see the movie *Love and Honor* in the theater. It all unfolded in my mind: We'd sneak away to the city on the bus, in the middle of the afternoon, when Saffiya was snoring inside and Bhaggan slept on her charpoy under the *shahtoot* tree.

I would wear Saffiya's earrings, the gold ones with little rubies that I had stolen. But I'd keep them covered with my dopatta, in case they were recognized as real gold and pulled from my earlobes. I'd stand behind Taaj at the ticket counter and let a glimpse of gold shine through to the man at the counter, proof that we were a legitimate couple.

He would be convinced of this as he handed the two tickets to Taaj.

I would blush.

Once in the theater, we'd sit close and I'd dig my fingers into my bra and pull out two rupees and hand them to him. "We can share a Coke and a samosa during the break," I would say. Then he'd smile and tell me to wait until the vendor came to us, so he wouldn't have to leave me by myself.

"Next time I'll bring you in a car," he would promise me.

I imagined sitting in the front seat of a car with him while he wove around the buffalo and camels on the streets, swerving to miss them, but the motion of the car would bring us closer. The radio would be playing "You've Stolen My Heart, Don't Steal My Life," or "How Does Spring Arrive Unannounced?" just like in the movies.

"Do you hear me?" Saffiya's shrieking pierced my ears. "Call Bhaggan. She's the only one who can talk some sense into you."

I walked out, still refusing to speak, hoping I wouldn't find her, but Bhaggan had prepared the tea tray and was waiting for me to bring it in.

"What, my daughter?" She looked at me as I walked into the kitchen, feeling the power of my silence dissipate.

I shrugged and picked up the tray, and then out of the corner of my eye caught her wiping her eyes with her dopatta. Did she feel my pain?

She shuffled behind me, bolstering my obstinacy, and sat in the corner near the entrance to Saffiya's room.

In contrast with my defiance, Bhaggan, a bundle of garlic and onion–smelling fabric, sat emanating the sweaty alarm in response to my insolence. Her drooping jowls forced me to acknowledge that Saffiya was still speaking. She wasn't going to let up. My mind was racing, but my body stagnated. I focused on Bhaggan, trying to ignore what I heard, but Saffiya's deep, jaded voice hammered into my mental silence.

"Bhaggan, you tell her. Does she have any other chance? Of course she doesn't. Here is an educated man. Someone who doesn't even care about her looks or her family. Someone who—"

"Bibi, there'll be others," Bhaggan inserted, as Saffiya choked on her words.

"I'm not asking you!" Saffiya shouted, as soon as she caught her breath again.

"Listen, Bibi," Bhaggan said, "give her some time."

I turned toward Bhaggan and glared at her. Did she really think I would give in?

Saffiya turned on Bhaggan. "This is all your doing. You've made her feel so special. Who is she, anyway? You know as well as I do, if it hadn't been for me telling you to brush away the flies, she would have been left there. Maybe that would have been what she wanted all along. Her mother must have been some kind of witch. I'm telling you. You should have had more sense. You were older than me. You knew what this would . . ." Saffiya placed her hand on her chest and then on her head, unable to breathe.

Bhaggan moved closer in a miserable attempt to help her benefactor and looked at me as I stood close to the tea tray, having just poured a cup for Saffiya. I picked up the cup and saucer and passed it to Saffiya. With a flip of her finger, Saffiya tipped the saucer and the teacup flew toward Bhaggan, hitting her on the shoulder. Milky liquid trickled over her breasts and into her lap, ending in a pool near the door.

Bhaggan took her dopatta from her head and wiped the tea off the floor. As she leaned over the entrance to clear the way, Taaj entered the room, barely avoiding stepping on his mother's worn hands.

"Bibi Saffiya, the maulvi is here to talk to you," he said, and looked at me as he spoke. Bhaggan looked at him and then at me. And pulled herself up with the door handle.

She couldn't know what I was thinking. But even if she did, I no longer cared. And if the maulvi thought he would be able to convince me to change my mind, it was clear that he didn't know me at all.

Fading Colors

I chose my time to escape, picked up the tea tray with exaggerated caution, and took it to the kitchen, only to drop it into the cement dishwashing basin on the floor. The lid of the small teapot rolled off and shattered into three pieces.

Saffiya's anger exploded through the rooms, reaching the kitchen in a futile attempt to further devastate me. "Break all my dishes, now. That's all you're worth."

I slumped on the low stool, filled my fist with straw and ashes, and began washing the dishes. The running water from the faucet would drain the water tank and drown out Saffiya's voice. The broken lid lay where it had fallen.

The streaming faucet splattered around me, dampening my clothes and my spirits. My choices were limited: I could stay and marry the nameless nephew, or I could leave the house, never to return. But where would I go? I had nowhere to turn.

Where did Taaj go when he left for days and sometimes months? When he returned, he was welcomed with a loving embrace and a hot meal. But he was a man, and he had a mother—two barriers I could never overcome.

I was like the beggar women leading isolated lives at the shrine, with no one to care for them. But at least they didn't have anyone to answer to. Could I be like them? I had some money that I had saved—granted, not much—and I also had the gold earrings. The money would pay for the bus ticket to the shrine. I would keep the earrings for emergencies.

At the shrine, food would be free. I could sleep like the beggars and the dervish in the courtyard of the shrine. I would need a blanket and a pillow, which I would hide under the banyan tree in the courtyard.

I would let my hair grow into snakes around my head, and after a while, no one would be able to recognize me anymore. My life would be free of dishwashing and housecleaning. Would that life of freedom be better than what Saffiya and Bhaggan were planning for me?

I continued staring at the pieces as the kitchen screen door opened and Taaj crept in, followed by the maulvi. The maulvi walked toward me, but I chose not to look up from the dishes. He bent over and stroked my head, and I shut my eyes, absorbing his care.

"How is my daughter? Be careful with that broken pottery. It doesn't take much for a scratch to inflame and become an abscess."

I held back my tears, still not looking at him, but mumbled a response.

The maulvi then followed Taaj into Saffiya's room. The sitting room was used only for larger events, like Eid celebrations, or for more formal discussions, like when the land tenants came to negotiate the rent with Bibi Saffiya. For a personal matter like this, Saffiya's room would provide the required privacy.

The only time Saffiya's room was off-limits for others was if the door was locked. Otherwise, she ate her meals there, and village folk and relatives gathered around her charpoy on folding chairs and high stools.

Every morning and early evening, Bhaggan sat herself down on Bibi Saffiya's bedroom floor and leaned against the wall, close enough to the door that she could hold on to the handle and lift herself up. There she sat, planning the meals of the day and discussing village politics.

That afternoon, Bhaggan had sat herself in her usual corner while Saffiya was having tea, to discuss the evening meal. I imagined that Taaj would have pulled in a folding chair to place near the entrance of the room, so that Maulvi could sit at a respectable distance from Saffiya.

He would have cleared his throat and, after wishing Saffiya a long and prosperous life, sat silently, waiting for Saffiya to ask, "So, what brings you here today, just a short while before the late-afternoon prayer call?"

I was confident that he had come to convince Saffiya not to follow through on the proposal to marry me to his wife's nephew. He might not even have told his wife before he'd come.

The maulvi knew his wife's nephew well. He knew he would not make a good husband for me. So maybe he was here to convince Saffiya and Bhaggan to wait for someone who had more to offer, someone who was young and good-looking. Bhaggan would remain silent, but I was sure Saffiya would mention her responsibility to find a suitable husband and home for me. She would remind him that that was her prime responsibility as my mother.

I imagined that he would agree and then softly persuade her that because of my intelligence and charm, and because of my connection with her family, a family well renowned in the area, there would be many, much more appealing young men who would want my hand in marriage. He would convince both of them that any hasty decisions would not only ruin my life but also ruin their reputations for knowing how to select who would become part of the household. I convinced myself that this was how it was unfolding. There could be no other reason for him to have come to see Saffiya.

This thought gave me hope as I finished washing the dishes. I picked up the broken teapot and placed the pieces together. I could use the extrastrong glue to piece them together.

Wiping my hands on my dopatta and filled with new hope, I tiptoed toward Saffiya's room and saw Taaj standing at the door.

He looked at me and placed his finger on his lips, indicating that I should remain silent. As I moved closer, I heard the end of what Saffiya was saying: "I'll give her nothing."

"That's all right, Bibi. Tara is a sensible girl. She's always been that way. Remember how she cared for Maria when Jannat couldn't. The girl will manage her life. I just wanted you to know the whole truth about the situation."

I was pleased. The maulvi knew his wife was as incompetent at matchmaking as she was at her other work. He would save me from this disastrous proposal. He was reassuring Saffiya that others would recognize my worth, like he did. I didn't have to be married to the first man who asked.

But the maulvi did not stop there.

"His problems are not minor. Even as a boy, he threw tantrums. When Zakia returned from her brother's village, she cried for her brother and his wife. They were tormented by their son's rage."

I had never heard the maulvi openly criticize someone. And this was his wife's nephew. He coughed and continued, "All the young women in his village turned down his marriage proposals, until they brought a girl from another village. But after two beatings, which landed her in the city hospital, the girl refused to return. They were never divorced."

Rage for Zakia welled up in me once more. She wanted me to be a second wife to such a brute.

Even more reason, I thought, for Saffiya and Bhaggan to tell the maulvi that his useless wife needed to be taught a lesson.

The silence emanating from the room smelled of doubt and guilt. I looked at Taaj to see if he sensed my relief, but he just shifted his weight from his left leg to the right. Taaj had never been a sensitive boy. He wasn't astute about his surroundings, so he must not have realized the direction the conversation was taking.

"Then . . . ," Saffiya said, and paused again. I could hear Bhaggan clear her throat and click her fingers loudly. But she, too, remained silent.

"Then," the maulvi continued, "you have to do what is best for her. She is like a daughter to you."

Why was it taking so long for her to reach a decision?

"It is nearly time for the late-afternoon prayer," the maulvi said. "I will have to go to the mosque to call for it. My legs are not as strong as they used to be, but I owed it to you to let you know. You have been kind to us. You have provided us with housing and money enough to fill our stomachs."

What, I thought, *has any of this got to do with my situation?*

"And Tara has always been very dear to me. She is like the daughter I never had. You know how Zakia and I have been praying to the Almighty to hear our one wish, but we must have committed an unforgivable sin."

Bhaggan spoke up now. "You and Zakia are both people of God," she said. "You led the funeral prayers for my husband and my son. I am also indebted to you and your wife. You have both taught my children everything they know about religion in this life and the next." She went on, "Ever since I've had any sense, I have been with Bibi Saffiya. And I know she trusts you like a family member."

Bhaggan was stating what Saffiya would never let pass through her own lips. She would never be beholden to anyone.

"But if you promise that you will take good care of her, I know Bibi Saffiya will never send you away empty-handed."

Now I was even more perplexed. Bhaggan wasn't making any sense.

The maulvi's response soon made things clearer: "Of course, I will personally keep him under my control. They will live in our home after they get married, and I will gain a grown daughter and a son. I have always considered Tara the daughter that I never had. Her husband will be like a son to me. Their children will be a blessing to us. They will open the doors of paradise for Zakia and me. We will not have lived our lives in vain."

More silence.

"Not to worry, Bibi Saffiya. Tara will still be close to you, as she is today. She can continue to serve you like a daughter during the day and keep old Amman Bhaggan company in the kitchen. Zakia will take care of their babies," the maulvi continued.

He had worked it all out. What kind of love was this?

"You crazy old man!" I wanted to shout. "Is this how you protect the ones you love? You were the only man who paid any attention to me as a child—who listened to me, who smiled at me, who gave me hope. For this? You deserve the bitter woman who is like a rock that drowns you in the canal. Your fate should be in the depths of the dark waters at night. You should be torn apart by the boar in the cane fields. You are worse than the others. At least they didn't give me reason to dream."

"In the evenings, she will be ours."

The dizziness of despair overpowered me. My eyes searched for stability from Taaj. His right ear twitched, but he didn't turn toward me.

A shuffling of shoes and feet from the room indicated that the meeting was nearly over, but I was not going to stay for the end. Hearing the decision would make it permanent.

I would pretend nothing had happened. I would go about my routine, and that would erase what I had heard.

I turned and walked toward the *shahtoot* tree. Saffiya's washed clothes would have dried by now. This time, the color would not fade in the sunlight.

It must be a mistake, I thought, as I walked toward the two trees. Had I just heard the maulvi try to convince Saffiya and Bhaggan that I should become the second wife of Zakia's nephew and live with them in the house in the village so that they could protect me when he lost his temper? Was that the only way to help me?

Was I that much of a burden to them? And why had Bhaggan remained silent? Did she agree with all this?

I gathered the brightly colored, still damp *shalwar kameezes* and threw them back in a pile on the charpoy. I didn't care about the white hand towels spread on the *chameli* bushes in the sun, now stiff with total dehydration but covered with small patches of dust from the leaves.

Returning to my routine and gathering the partially dried clothes to clarify my confusing thoughts did not help me. It didn't take me long to realize that I needed to torment them all by controlling my own life.

A Frog Underfoot

⟡⟡⟡⟡⟡

The heat of anger vaporized my tears, leaving a starchy itchiness in my eyes. I wiped my face with my dopatta and sat on the edge of the charpoy under the trees. The sun dissolved into the distant fields and emanated a torrid heat. The fields stood motionless, but the sky above was melting.

On any other day at this time, Bhaggan would have been waking from her afternoon nap on the veranda, but the commotion about my future had prevented that. When Maria and I had been younger, Bhaggan's siesta had been our time for freedom. She had awoken ignorant to our stolen joy, but since she had also been refreshed, no one had complained. The beginning of the evening was usually a time for rejuvenation in preparation for the cooler night winds, but today the heat had stagnated us.

All those years ago, the day Sultan had died, Maria and I had married our dolls. She had told me how the boy doll lay on top of the girl. How many months later the baby would be born. Maria's knowledge had angered me then, but it had made me more curious.

Later, if the topic ever came up, I would lean forward to listen in on the village women's hushed conversations, in hopes of knowing more, only to be met with silence. They stopped midsentence, sensing I was eavesdropping on conversations that were not for my young ears. How would I ever know what happened when men and women got married?

I couldn't think of whom to ask. This frustrated me further.

I had no idea what would happen if I married Zakia's nephew. For the most part, the village women had talked of fear and pain with marriage. Very few mentioned pleasure.

Now, I wished for anyone, even Maria, to tell me that I would not be the second wife of the man who had beaten his first wife so hard that she had never returned to him. That I would not have to live in Zakia's house and continue working as a servant my whole life.

Saffiya's damp clothes lay on the charpoy in front of me. I stared at them, not wanting to do anything with them.

The late-afternoon prayer called to the villagers. The maulvi had reached the mosque, no doubt pleased that he had gained a daughter who would bear children to keep him company in his old age.

I was brought out of my reverie by a proposal very different from the one I was trying to avoid.

"I can take you to see the movie tomorrow." I wasn't sure how long Taaj had been standing there. He must have ushered the maulvi out and then come out here.

I stayed seated and looking toward the fields. I could see a tiny figure in the distance. I wondered who it was. Could it be Maalik returning from the cane fields, where he had found work making sugar in those large fire pits? Often he stayed in the one-room hovel, keeping watch over the equipment.

"You'll still be here," Taaj said, trying to console me. Why couldn't he understand? I didn't just want to stay here and have things be the same as always. I wanted things to change. I wanted them to be better.

He moved closer to me. The sweat emanating from his body embraced me. My thoughts blurred, but my intentions were now clear. I would not let anyone control my life. I would do what my mother must have done.

I lay back on the charpoy and looked up at him. I took his hand and tugged him toward me. He looked confused, but I knew now what I would do.

The charpoy creaked as I pulled him on top of me, and his chest covered mine. I breathed deeply and felt a warmth fill me. I was overwhelmed by ripples of euphoria I had never experienced before. Waves of this ecstasy engulfed me, and I wanted them to continue forever.

I shut my eyes and sighed with pleasure. He moved his body on top of mine and began panting. I could feel parts of his body that I knew I shouldn't feel so close to mine. I wondered if he could sense what I thought, but his gasps seemed to have taken over his body and mind. I decided to stop thinking myself and let my body control my mind. There was so much pleasure in that. A freedom that I had not anticipated.

He looked at me again but remained silent. Confidence had replaced his confusion. He smiled at me.

Anyone could have seen us on the charpoy, but no one was close enough. We both knew that it wouldn't be long before someone came looking for me, so I pushed him off me and pulled myself off the charpoy. A half-dead fly fell to the hardened ground as I shook the clothes to straighten them. I stepped on it to relieve it of its misery.

Taaj began walking toward the alfalfa fields behind the trees and turned to look at me. He didn't have to beckon me to follow. I'd already made up my mind. The crop was now knee-high. I knew I had to follow him. I left the laundered clothes on the charpoy.

I was more aware of my surroundings than of my thoughts. The sun had begun to descend, but steam emanated from the fields. Our landscape dissolved as Taaj pulled me down beside him and lay on top of me.

My feeling of euphoria began to dissipate as he pulled at my *shalwar*. Panic reared inside me. I had lost the pleasure I'd felt a few minutes earlier on the charpoy. I stretched out my hands, unsure of my own actions. I pressed my hands into the ground to propel myself up but ended up with fists full of dirt. A rock stabbed into my back, and my right foot squished something, maybe a frog.

And then something shifted, and again my mind relinquished its power to my body. Taaj's greasy hair was bobbing above my head. I was choosing to be controlled by him. A few mosquitoes buzzed over his left shoulder and distracted me. Beyond the mosquitoes, the sky was turning a deep purple and I could see a few very dim pinpricks of stars.

I thought I said something, but I wasn't sure who I was addressing or what I was saying, and since Taaj didn't respond, it might have been my imagination. His panting became frantic. I might have pushed him away, but my memory is unclear. A searing pain tore me, and I wanted to shout. Maybe I did, but it didn't make a difference. He kept moving. He kept hurting me.

And then it was all over.

There was silence. And he was no longer on top of me.

I could see the sky more clearly now, and it had grown darker. The mosquitoes had disappeared, but somewhere in the distance I saw a firefly. It blinked a few times.

I don't know when Taaj left my side. I only remember returning to the charpoy under the *shahtoot* tree and picking up the now-dry clothes and returning to the kitchen and seeing Amman Bhaggan preparing the evening meal.

"Where have you been, my child?"

Could she know? I thought. I remained silent.

"I needed help with the onions."

I held the bundle of clothes in one hand, straightened my dopatta with the other, and walked into another room.

"You can get some rags from under my bed," she said.

And I didn't know why I would need them, since I'd just had my monthly bleeding two weeks earlier.

Solace

A dull glow spread across the horizon as I walked toward Maria's house in the village. Darkness and the night wails of hyenas followed close behind. I was waking up into a nightmare of my own creation. I realized why Bhaggan had thought my monthly bleeding had started. The pain I had felt with Taaj had injured me, and she had seen the bloodstain on my *kameez*. I should have changed my clothes before returning to the kitchen. The mud stains on my back from lying in the field would not have alerted her as much as the blood evoking my impurity for the week.

I had left the clean laundry outside Saffiya's room in a pile, and before I could be called to iron it or do any other petty chore for her, I decided to find Maria. I wouldn't tell her everything I had done, but I needed her to help calm me down so I could think clearly, to get myself out of the mess of marrying an imbecile.

Maria rarely came to Saffiya's house anymore, now that Stella had left. She spent more time with her parents. I never knew how she could stand to spend countless hours with her complaining mother, but she kept their one-room home spotless and cooked all the meals.

I needed Maria now.

I had defied my elders and knew there would be a price to pay. As I walked, the soreness inside me became more pronounced. How could I have lost control of my own body in that way? How could I have let what had happened transpire? Had I asked for it? And if I was seeking out Maria now, whom would Taaj tell about what we had done? I tried to piece it all together.

I couldn't recall past the frog under my foot and the deepening sky above me and Taaj's head and then the pain. The sharp pain. How had the pleasant beginning ended in such agony? I wondered if I had started something that would grow to overshadow my whole life. Why had I not given it more thought?

Maybe it was Taaj's fault and not mine. Could I blame him? I had wanted him to do something, and I hadn't even known what it was or where it would take me. But he should have known. He would have known. Taaj had never cared much for anyone other than himself.

I began to pick up my pace as I became more alert. In the silence of the night, I heard the distant drone of buses on the main road and thought of Taaj. He had said nothing to me before we parted. I, too, had been silent.

He must have bolted in the opposite direction to the house. He would have scampered past the cane fields, outrunning the wild boar, and scrambled over the canal bridge, scaring the snakes slithering beneath it. He would have reached the main road by the time I had returned to the kitchen. There, he would have jumped onto the first bus heading toward the coolness of the mountains, away from the heat of the flatlands.

As with all the previous times he had disappeared, he would be gone for a while, only to be missed by his mother, wondering and worrying about where his next meal would come from and where he would rest for the night. He would no doubt return. Maybe in a week, maybe in a month, or maybe, this time, in a few years.

But I knew I should stop thinking about him, because even if he were thinking of me, he was gone. He had left me. We might have shared that brief intimacy, but he wasn't going to admit to his share of guilt. He would say I had enticed him. Bhaggan had always told me that women led men astray. Men had weak minds and strong bodies. Women had weak bodies but strong minds. Had I proven her right?

I had to think about myself. About what I had done. What we had done. There would be consequences. But who knew what?

My confusion was bubbling over and steaming up my thoughts. I would explode like the pressure cooker Bhaggan had hidden behind the flour drum, for fear of another explosion. It had taken me a whole day to clean the pieces of meat spattered on the wall, and even months later, I had found desiccated bone fragments behind the lentil boxes in the far corner of the kitchen.

Taaj was gone, and I would have to clean up.

By the time I reached Maria's house, darkness had enveloped me. As if sensing my arrival, the bare lightbulb hanging outside the front door lit up, and as I opened the door without even knocking, the aroma of freshly baked bread greeted me.

In the courtyard, Maria was seating herself in front of the stove, having just turned on the light switch.

She looked up as I entered, and I held back my tears. She would not see me cry.

She pushed back the stool, stood up quickly, and began

walking toward me, now that I had lost the energy to move any farther.

She hugged me, and my hands fell limply to my sides. She took my right hand and pulled me toward the charpoy in the courtyard and sat me down. Still holding my hand, she sat next to me.

I needed her to be the Maria who couldn't stop talking, but she wasn't, and maybe I respected this new Maria more. She stroked my hand and looked at me.

"I'm waiting for my meal!" Jannat called from inside the room.

"Okay, Mother. Give me a few minutes. It's nearly ready." She didn't tell her mother about my arrival.

I whispered to Maria, "You know the night we went to the canal to hear the babies cry?" She said nothing, and I couldn't continue.

Her mother coughed. Maria got up and prepared a plate of spicy potatoes and roti and took it in to her. She then made another plate and brought it to the charpoy where I sat. She made a morsel and placed it in my mouth, and I began to chew. Then she put one in her own mouth, and we shared the meal until she wiped the plate clean.

"I know how much you hate washing dishes. Now I've made it easy for you," Maria said. Then she smiled. "Don't worry. I wasn't going to ask you to wash it." I couldn't answer, as it took all my effort to hold back my tears.

"Who's there? Who are you talking to at this time of the evening?" Jannat shouted from within.

"No one, Amman. It's just Tara. She came from Bibi Saffiya's house to ask after you."

"She's never cared for me before. Did she bring my wages?"

"Not today," Maria responded.

I couldn't trust myself to speak. Not yet.

Maria returned to her mother to take her empty plate. Her mother's voice emanated from within. "Your father will need a plate."

"No, Amman. Not tonight. He went to the shrine tonight. He will eat there and sleep there, too. He has gone for blessings."

"What blessings has he got that haven't reached us?" Jannat responded, and Maria busied herself with washing the dishes.

I got up from the charpoy to help her.

"What would Bibi Saffiya say if she knew we ate from the same plate?" She laughed.

"I've done much worse than that today," I responded.

She looked at me questioningly. "You?"

So I told her. I told her how my marriage was being arranged and how I had chosen to respond. She kept washing the dishes and wiping them and putting them away, but she heard me.

"Now what?"

"Zakia will no longer want me to marry her nephew." At least there was some good news to come from all of this.

"How will she know what happened?"

I sat silent. I hadn't thought that far. A heaviness began to descend on me again. I had taken a step, a leap. I had crossed a chasm, only to be surrounded by quicksand. I was sinking.

"Who will you tell? Amman Bhaggan? Bibi Saffiya? They will tell you to stay silent. And then your *nikah* will be done to Zakia's nephew sooner than anyone had expected."

When had Maria become smarter than I?

I stood up and then sat down again.

"I need tea." Jannat's voice sounded sleepier now.

"What does your mother do inside all day?" I asked Maria in a whisper, choosing not to answer her question.

"She comes out during the day, but in the evening she stays on her charpoy. And she dreams. She says her babies come to her at night, looking for her. One day she said Stella had also come, and that scared me. But I reminded her that we had received a letter from her just a week earlier and that she was all right."

She moved the embers in the stove and kindled a new fire to make some tea. I stared into the sparks, looking for a way to escape. My mind was searching for ways that I had seen or heard about. What had other village women done? What had I seen in the movies and soaps on TV?

"Will Amman Bhaggan wonder where you are?" Maria asked.

"Probably." Outwardly, I was calm, but the smoke of the dung fire had seeped inside me, blurring my thoughts. I didn't want to admit to Maria that I had not anticipated my quandary.

"But Maalik usually returns from the fields at this time and sits with her. He doesn't say much. She makes him his dinner while he smokes. I usually go in to massage Saffiya and watch my favorite soaps on TV." I looked around at the simple surroundings. "How can you spend your evening here without a radio or a TV?" I asked.

"Stella has sent me some picture books that I try to read, but I'm usually so exhausted that I go to sleep just after sunset."

"Are you telling me to leave now?" I responded, knowing what I would do.

The fire was now burning brightly, and the smoke and ashes in the air had cleared.

"Never." She was the devoted Maria I knew.

Though I had to return, my burden was lighter now. The feeling of dread that had weighted me down as I'd come to my friend had lifted significantly.

Moonlight illuminated my path. Two stray dogs settled into a pile of sand on the roadside, barely noticing me. As I neared the house, I could see the maulvi walk toward the mosque to call for the late-evening prayer.

SIX MILES LEFT

Chosen Destiny

Two pairs of honey-colored eyes looked up at me as I entered the kitchen, one exhausted and the other agitated.

As with most evenings, Maalik and Bhaggan sat on the *peerhis* close to the ground, their plates on the floor, eating their evening meal. But the meal was half-finished, as if they had been deep in conversation.

Maalik was like his eldest brother, Sultan. He talked less and tried hard, but he never did well in school. As a result, he'd dropped out to work in the fields in the mornings and care for the buffalo in the evenings. He corralled them to the canal with his navigational stick and then brought them home before it got dark. At night he placed his charpoy close to them to guard them from dacoits.

Unlike his older brother Taaj, he did not watch movies, but he also never joined the maulvi at the mosque for prayers, as Sultan had done.

"He's gone again." Bhaggan sighed. "My poor Taaj. I don't know what haunts him here so that he cannot stay. He says life stands still here and he has to move on. Before he knows it, his aging mother will have moved on." She wiped her eyes with her dopatta, but Maalik kept staring at me.

I could never guess what Maalik was thinking. He kept his emotions to himself, unlike his mother or even his brother Taaj. Even when Sultan had died, he had sat stone-faced, staring at the mourners. I didn't think much of this behavior even now.

"Maalik said he saw him leaving, just before sunset. Why would he leave at night like a robber? Why wouldn't he wait till the morning and say farewell and take my blessings with him?"

She picked up the half-finished plates and passed them to me. "Here, my daughter. Wash these plates for me. We are both too worried to finish our meal. I made a plate for you, too. It's lying near the stove, covered with the bread cloth."

I busied myself washing the plates with my back to them, but I could feel Maalik's stare as I sat hunched at the faucet. I then picked up the plate she had made for me and placed it in the fridge. My shared meal with Maria had been enough for the night.

"Take it out of the fridge before Saffiya sees it. You know how she hates to see our food in there. Last time, she threw away a whole plate of my daal in the sink," Bhaggan cautioned me, and added, "She's already upset that you left her clothes wrinkled in a ball outside her room."

Bhaggan pulled herself up, holding the cabinet to steady herself. "Where were you, anyway? She wants to talk to you."

I feigned ignorance of why Saffiya would want to talk to me. I was no longer certain about what I would do, so I returned to my tactic of avoidance.

"Jannat wasn't feeling well," I lied. "I went to help Maria."

"That poor, crazy woman. For Maria, she'll have to find a husband who'll live with them. How will she manage if Maria leaves?"

The talk of Maria's marriage chafed at the soreness of my own dilemma. Inflammation grew, creating pain and panic. How would I get out of it? The old hag was making it worse.

Slamming the kitchen door as I left, I went outside to breathe under the first stars of the night. I needed a clear mind and silence to sift through the debris of the day.

I perched myself on the low brick wall surrounding the garden and looked up for a sign of respite. A flashing star flew across the sky, and I heard the sound of youthful footsteps approaching. Maalik must have followed me.

I had never talked much to Maalik. His presence was peripheral to my existence and had never moved closer. I never felt compelled to engage in conversation, and, apparently, neither did he.

He acted strange. Either he would talk too much and not let others interrupt, or he would remain silent and we would never know what he was thinking. Only Bhaggan had long conversations with him, but you couldn't really call them conversations. She would talk and talk, and he would respond with a word or two.

So he surprised me when it seemed as if he wanted to connect with me. Was he responding to my despair?

He stood silently behind me for a while and then, in a barely audible whisper, said, "Everything. I saw."

My shoulders stiffened. I covered my head with my dopatta and chose not to respond. He had been that distant figure as I had laid myself on the charpoy. What exactly had he seen? Would I use him as the harbinger of my deeds to Zakia and the maulvi? If he told his mother, she would keep it to herself; so would Saffiya. Then, as Maria had guessed, they would plan a quick *nikah*, and before I knew it, I would be living in Zakia's house with her dreaded nephew.

And, as if sensing my thoughts, he added, "I didn't tell, but Taaj is gone, again."

Did he think Taaj had left because of what we had done?

He seemed strangely calm. I wasn't sure whether he was chastising me or supporting me. Before he could clarify, in my defense, I blurted, "Do you know what they're planning for me? That good-for-nothing scoundrel, Zakia's nephew—"

He didn't let me finish. "You have to marry someone."

His calm infuriated me. "But not him!"

He took a cigarette box from his pocket. "Bring me a match."

I'm not going in again, I thought.

"Amman's in Saffiya's room. They'll talk till late."

I turned around to look at him, but the moon had risen, creating a bright halo around him and darkening his face so I couldn't decipher his thoughts.

"Only if you let me have one, too," I dared him, and returned with a box with three matches. "You'll have to make these work. Your mother counts the matches. She'll wonder where they went."

He lit the cigarette, took a puff, and passed it to me.

Bhaggan used to let me puff on her hookah on winter evenings when I sat massaging her tired shoulders. Both Taaj and Maalik had seen her sharing it with me and didn't think much of my taking a few turns on the cigarettes so dear to them.

I wondered if Sultan had ever smoked. I had never seen him with a cigarette.

Again, I sensed Maalik entering my mind. How much did he really understand about the situation? How was he the only one of all three brothers who seemed to know my situation? "He was the best of the three of us. He wouldn't have done what Taaj did to you. And if he had, he would have married you first."

Blood rushed to my face, but he continued not to look at me. "He would never have given you a cigarette, either," he said, retrieving it from me, holding it with a finger and a thumb, and taking a long puff.

The cigarette lit up his face, and as he blew a long stream of smoke and narrowed his eyes, I wondered why he was bringing up his brother, who had been dead now for so many years.

"It was ugly the day he died. You know what the maulvi did? He asked me, not Taaj. Taaj couldn't stand the horror. He asked me, the youngest, to help bathe that dead body. A body that was not even whole. A body with the intestines showing. The bus. It had done something. To the stomach. You've seen the slaughtered cows, haven't you?"

I wanted him to stop. He was making me feel sick. Why was he telling me all this?

He stared at me, as if daring me to defy his strength. After a few moments, his eyelids drooped and the stare began to glaze over. His voice seemed to come from somewhere deep within him. A place that was not under his full control.

"And then you know what the maulvi said? He said I couldn't tell anyone. He said it was wrong to tell anyone about this sacred ritual."

I heard a bus in the distance, and then closer, probably near the village, a dog whined as if something or someone had hit it.

"Sultan would have made a good husband," he continued, in the same monotonous tone, while he puffed on his cigarette. "Sometimes when I stay guarding the buffalo at night, or when I sit in that room in the middle of the cane fields, I think of him. And think of our father. He was a good husband, too.

That's what Amman thinks. But he died before I was born. That means I didn't really have a father." He puffed some more on the cigarette, until he reached the butt, and then he sucked on it, taking in the magic that gave him strength to vocalize his thoughts. This was the first time I had heard him lead a conversation, and I wondered what had encouraged him.

Then, as if the power of the cigarette needed to be bolstered, he dug into his pocket and pulled out a bidi, wrapped in dried leaves. "This is better," he said, as he lit it, sucked on it, and handed it to me.

I took a puff, not knowing how it would affect me, but by now I didn't care.

Maalik took the bidi back and continued smoking it, pausing briefly to add, "So, you don't have a mother. And I don't have a father. Maybe I should marry you."

The moon had risen higher in the sky and shone directly on his face. Or maybe he had moved. Or maybe I had moved. I wasn't clear about what was happening. Was it only that afternoon that the maulvi had come to finalize my marriage plans? When I had decided to take my fate into my own hands? But it still evaded me. And now Maalik was giving me a way out. I could escape the destiny that others had chosen for me. I could create my own.

We sat in silence until the bidi was finished. Something shuffled beneath the *chameli* bush. The white buds would bloom the next morning. Through the haze and darkness, they looked like flies in white funeral shrouds. I was back in that morning. The morning of the *chameli* garland. Of the snake scare. Of the pretend wedding. Of the violent death of Sultan.

The smoke and the fumes built up bile in my mouth. I didn't know where to turn, so I threw up the potatoes and roti that Maria had shared with me on the *chameli* bush.

The Truth

I never tried a bidi again after that night. The pungent smell sickened me to my core and reminded me of a memory that left me bewildered. Later, I learned that Maalik's bidis were made not of tobacco and leaves, but rather of a concoction that apparently helped him think straight but confused the rest of us.

Maalik's altered bidi added to my sensation of stumbling into a bottomless abyss, my control over my life receding as I fell, but his proposal was like a bucket that scraped me as it was dropped down the well to save me. I would no longer be spending my life with Zakia as a mother-in-law and a husband who would cause me bodily harm. I had been rescued from a death of drowning in verbal and physical abuse. Like Bhaggan, I would live a long life and bear children who would care for me. My mind was still swimming in the murkiness the bidi caused, but I could, at least, breathe. At last, I would escape the burden of an unhappy marriage.

I answered his proposal with silence, which he interpreted as agreement, as did I. This was what I wanted. Bhaggan would be my mother-in-law. She knew me. She wouldn't expect anything different than how I had behaved all my life. She would continue to treat me like a daughter.

As for Maalik, I could live with him. He had also known me all my life. We had rarely played together, but that didn't matter. And he didn't seem to mind what I had done with Taaj. He probably also didn't remember that morning I had tried to entice Sultan to pin the *chameli* garland onto my hair.

A buzzing around my head distracted me from my ruminations about marriage. I thought it was a mosquito, attracted by the stickiness of sweat and oil. I brushed it away with my right hand, but the sound remained for a while and was then accompanied by a dull, putrid smell.

The bug landed on a piece of dung on the ground in front of me. Taaj had brought the buffalo this way, and they had deposited a load of dung. The bug hovered around the dung and then began rolling it into a ball. Maria and I had been terrified of these bugs when we were younger. Whenever we'd seen them roll the dung while we'd sat with Jannat to make dung cakes for cooking fuel, we'd started screaming. But my fear was now dead.

The bug worked hard. The dung ball grew, and the bug rolled it away under a large rock. I waited for it to return, but it must have gotten its fill.

I stayed outside after the bug had scuttled on, but now I began watching the stars change shape. I sought out the North Star, which seemed to appear in every direction. I heard a jackal scuttle around, making the sounds of day. The night flowers spread their aroma in worship of the sliver of moon, as if it were the sun. No human sounds of prayer emanated from the mosque at that time of night.

THE NEXT MORNING, after I had made breakfast, Saffiya and Bhaggan called me into Saffiya's room to tell me what they had planned. I wondered what Maalik had shared with his mother the night before. He never lied, but what was the truth he had told her?

Neither of my mothers seemed upset with me. Saffiya was in charge. She knew what needed to happen, and Bhaggan sat silently. She never looked up at me, and I wondered why. Wouldn't she be happy to have me as her daughter-in-law? She had always appreciated the way I cared for her, had wanted a daughter like me.

"I'll call the maulvi this evening, and he will do your *nikah* with Maalik, and then you'll be married and my responsibilities will be complete. There's no need to invite anyone."

Maalik must have decided to tell Bhaggan that he wanted to marry me without telling her the reason why. I wondered why she hadn't suggested I marry Taaj or Sultan earlier. Had Zakia asked for my hand so soon that she had caught Bhaggan off guard? Why had she hesitated in asking for it first?

Even Saffiya had not suggested that I marry Bhaggan's sons. It would have been so convenient. I would have stayed in the house of my birth and continued to serve them both. But I had also never thought of marrying either of the two brothers. Granted, Sultan had seemed appealing when I was younger, but I also wanted to leave this house. That was how I could have released myself from the fate that I seemed to have bound to as soon as I had been found on that train. The fate that came with Bhaggan's wiping off the flies and feeding me the lump of raw cane sugar.

But now we had all reconciled. Saffiya announced my marriage with Maalik, not knowing that I had already shown my agreement to marry him. She didn't seem angry with me, but she was upset by the turn of events.

She fidgeted, picking up the spittoon that sat beside her

bed, before putting it down without spitting in it. She straightened the pillow that she was leaning on and then picked up the flyswatter, even though the fly she could see was out of her reach and she knew it. She tried to swat it from a distance, but it was oblivious to her irritation, none of which was directed toward me. I wondered how Maalik had accomplished this.

Bhaggan was also more animated than usual. She seemed to have forgotten her despair over Taaj's disappearance the night before. She sat on the floor near the door, in her usual place in Saffiya's room, but her manner was not the same. Usually during her daily meetings with Saffiya, she rarely moved from her position, but that morning she kept shifting her legs, unable to find a comfortable position.

I thought I knew both of these women well, but I couldn't understand their reaction to my situation. Wasn't Bhaggan happy that I would marry Maalik?

"Nah, Bibi!" she interrupted Saffiya. "Since Sultan died, this is the first time I will see happiness. I know Taaj has left us for a while and might not return to share his brother's joy, but at least let the village girls sing some wedding songs. Let me cook a special meal. I'll sacrifice a goat and make a large cauldron of saffron curry for the villagers."

Did that mean she was ready to celebrate our union, even though it was rushed? I wasn't sure what she would say to the villagers. How would she explain that just a day before, she had been helping to arrange my marriage with Zakia's nephew, and overnight she had decided to marry me to her younger son?

I stood in front of Saffiya, listening silently to her and Bhaggan continue to plan my fate as if I were still the foundling covered in flies. But, unbeknownst to them, it was a fate that I had helped create. It was a small victory for me, but I would relish it in silence.

Saffiya picked up the spittoon again and this time shot a load of spittle into it. Then she angrily wiped the excess moisture from her lips with the back of her hand and said, "That daughter of an owl, *uloo ki pathi*, how dare she? And I had put so much trust in her. She's a nobody, that Zakia, and she thought she'd send her husband . . . and he comes and sits here, in my room, and has the gall to tell me he will treat Tara like his daughter, will bring up their children as if they were his own. He sits for so long, making the whole village late for the late-afternoon prayer, pretending his wife's nephew is a man who can conceive children. There's no way he couldn't have known. Wasn't the man married to his cousin? Didn't she leave him and never return? If Maalik hadn't told us, we would have fallen into their trap."

I needed to know more. "Why, Bibi? What happened?" I blurted out. What had Maalik said to his mother? Did he know something that I didn't?

"Let's not dwell on it," Bhaggan was quick to respond. She didn't look at me.

"Tell her, Bhaggan. She needs to know the truth. Zakia pretends to be a woman of God, but here she was, trying to make us arrange Tara's marriage to a man who doesn't even enjoy the company of women. If Maalik hadn't told us about his preference for men, you would have been doomed. Zakia would have made me the laughingstock of the village. But why?"

"Maalik, may he have a long life, told me last night that he had met a man from the boy's first wife's village. The man had come to the canal to water his buffalo. Maalik got talking to him, and he said the wife chose never to marry again. She was traumatized by how he hadn't even touched her. Zakia's family said it was the girl's fault that she couldn't conceive, but everyone has seen the man with other men, holding hands, spending time with them, even after he got married," Bhaggan explained to the infuriated Saffiya.

Spittle continued to fly over Saffiya's bed as her anger increased on hearing the details. She wiped her mouth with her dopatta.

"What was their enmity against me?" Saffiya continued to question. "I have always been a well-wisher for everyone in the village. You know that, Bhaggan. You, Jannat, and Zakia have all been on my payroll, and I have compensated you all handsomely. I provide housing. I buy you all new outfits every Eid. And this is how I am repaid? By being tricked into marrying my adopted daughter to a man who is not even a man?"

Bhaggan's explanation didn't seem very calming. "The maulvi didn't want a dowry, but Zakia knows you are a rich woman. You would have given them more than she has seen in her life. I never trusted her. Even on Eid, when I sent them the sacrificial meat, she would ask for extra. She's greedy that way. Never satisfied. May Allah bless Maalik," Bhaggan repeated. "He's saved us all from infamy. He will marry Tara, and no one will expect a dowry from you."

Then she looked at me to clarify the gravity of the situation. "Maalik will give you a home, and Bibi Saffiya's good name will never be tarnished. She will keep her daughter in her protection by marrying you to Maalik."

I looked into her eyes, trying to decipher the truth of this story. Had Maalik really known this about Zakia's nephew but chosen not to tell me when he proposed?

Having resolved the reason for the maulvi and Zakia's deception, the two remained silent, collecting their thoughts, and then Saffiya spoke, as if to herself: "And I don't know why I hadn't thought of Maalik. Taaj, maybe, but Maalik?"

Her tone indicated doubt about the direction we would be taking, but then, within the same breath, her opinion changed.

"Some might say he's simple, but Maalik works hard. Speaks less. He can add another charpoy to the quarter in the fields near the canal. He takes the buffalo there anyway. You can live there. It's close enough, and you can come here daily."

She was now at her best. She would fix this problem in such a way that the resolution would be even better than expected. Forgetting me, the main reason for all the excitement, she turned to Bhaggan, her partner for the past twenty-five years, and began to plan my wedding.

So, Maalik didn't care about what I had done with his brother and Bhaggan didn't know about it? No one would ever know. But that still didn't explain why Bhaggan seemed distant. If my situation was now resolved, I would marry Maalik. And he was the simple one, so why was she not happy? She had shown more pleasure the day I had made my first round roti in the tandoor. Having me care for her as a daughter for the rest of her life should have made her ecstatic. Saffiya seemed contained and continued her planning.

"We can wait a few weeks. There's no rush. It'll serve Zakia right. She thought she could make a fool of me. I'll sacrifice a buffalo. Later today, you can help me bring my bridal trunk from the storage rooms. Hamida's mother can adjust my pink satin outfit with gold embroidery for the wedding day and the green satin one for the day after. The colors will look good on Tara, even if she isn't as pretty as I was then."

Bhaggan didn't disagree, and I said nothing. I had seen the outfits just a few months earlier, when she'd been airing out the mothball smell from her marriage trunks. Both outfits had sweat stains under the arms from so many years ago, when Saffiya had last worn them, before I was even born. When she had been bundled off to a husband chosen for her. To the house where she had borne no children and lived with a man who had died within the year.

Both outfits were better than any I had worn in my life, but I wanted a new one for my wedding day. One like I had seen on the bride on the TV show. I could never tell the color that the bride was wearing, because the TV colors were always a blurry gray, but I knew I wanted to be dressed like a princess on my wedding day, and those outfits didn't look very royal.

Mortar and Pestle

I had always imagined myself wearing a fiery red flowing *kameez* over a wide-bottomed *gharara*, like a princess. It would trail behind me. Maria and Hamida would help keep it straight when I walked toward the bridal stage and sat beside my groom. The groom would be dressed in a straight gold coat with a garland of five-rupee notes around his neck. On his head, he would wear a turban wrapped around a gold skullcap with the starched point reaching the heavens. The village women would sing wedding songs to the beat of the drum:

"Your tall and handsome groom / The envy of all the girls / May he be delivered from the evil eye."

I could never picture his face because it would be hidden behind a garland of roses and *chameli* and a few sparkles of tinsel. My own face would be hidden under my red veil, covered with fine gold embroidery. I would sit myself beside him and place my paisley-hennaed hands tidily on my lap, and the guests would crowd around us in admiration, giving us our wedding gifts of money. They would joke about what we were expected to do that night, without saying anything that would offend the older guests.

After the marriage dinner, Maria would bring a mirror for

our first glimpse of each other as husband and wife. We would glance shyly in the mirror without looking directly at each other, in case, unintentionally, of course, we cast an evil eye on our happiness.

Then Hamida's mother, a happily married woman with healthy children, would bring a sweet to my lips for me to taste and receive the same blessings. And then my groom would be expected to take a bite from the same section that I had bitten into, indicating our eternal love for each other. The people around us would laugh knowingly, and in embarrassment I would bend my head even lower.

When it was time to leave, my handsome groom's best friend would sit beside him. Hamida would sit at our feet to straighten my gown and would steal my groom's shoe to stall our departure. If he wanted to leave with me, he would have to pay her money. The crowd would join in the argument over how much money to pay before he could take his bride and leave.

I would smile under my dopatta, knowing that his friend had already decided on an amount but would give a few rupees while the crowd around us shouted their disagreement at such a small sum. The bargaining would continue until Bhaggan or Hamida's mother said, "That's enough, now. It's getting late. Let them go."

Unfortunately, Saffiya's plans for my wedding did not match my fantasy. And no one thought of including me in any of the wedding plans. It was like me organizing my dolls' wedding.

"I will give her my earrings and a forehead pendant. And maybe even a nose ring. You can give her your gold bangle, the one your husband gave you. I have it in my closet. That's it, Bhaggan. Spend the next two weeks in preparation, and then we will cook a feast for the whole village."

Was she going to be looking for the earrings that I had already taken? What an uproar there would be when she realized they were no longer in the packet on top of the Quran. But I would worry about that later. I had no intention of putting them back where I'd found them.

Saffiya was planning to spend more than I had anticipated. She intended to open her purse strings, like a loving mother. A buffalo was a tremendous cost. I knew because when one of the villagers' buffalo had been attacked by a boar and died without time for it to be slaughtered to eat, the whole village had mourned. The wailing women who had enticed Bhaggan to wail when Sultan had died had been brought in to mourn for the family. They had been inconsolable. Even Saffiya had sent her condolences.

Then Saffiya added, "Bhaggan, do you want me to take some of the expenses out of your pay? He *is* your son."

Bhaggan sat silent and then said, "Whatever you think is appropriate."

I could see that she was now dejected, but they continued their planning without consulting me. Tired of standing, and not wanting to massage Saffiya that morning, I sat on the floor next to Bhaggan. I pulled at my toenails, half listening to what would happen on my special day.

I was glad that I was being ignored, because I could focus on the circumstances that had brought me here: my actions of the day before, and how they would change what was to come.

Maalik had his strange ways. He could never hold back the truth, even at the expense of others' displeasure. I didn't doubt what he had told his mother about Zakia's nephew. Despite his truth saying, he was never able to look anyone in the eye, even if the other person was the only one in the room. And he never reacted to a situation in the expected way. But I also knew he cared. He cared for his mother. He had cared for Sultan. And everyone knew that he cared for the buffalo more than anything else.

He would care for me, too. He hadn't gotten me in trouble, as he could have. In fact, he was the only one who was helping me escape. I felt the warmth inside me grow. It felt good.

Maalik might have been considered different, but who wouldn't have been if he had had to wash his dead brother's body for burial rites? So what if he didn't talk too much? A silent house was a happy house.

I smiled to myself and then realized the room around me was now quiet. I sensed tension but didn't know why, as I hadn't been following the conversation. I wondered what the disagreement between the two women had been.

Amman Bhaggan was pulling herself off the floor with the door handle, and Saffiya had picked up the spittoon again. I looked at both of them, but they were not going to share their thoughts with me.

I followed Bhaggan to the kitchen, where she had already started preparing the afternoon meal. She didn't ask me to peel the onions or wash the meat, but I knew what had to be done, so I started preparing the garlic and added the spices to the mortar and ground them silently to make paste for the curry, softening the aroma of garlic with coriander.

Bhaggan started the fire with kindling left over from the previous night, and, without her having to tell me, I went outside and filled my dopatta with dung cakes to build the fire in both stoves. She placed the dung cakes in each stove and then balanced a pot on each.

I waited for her to say something, to ask me to pass the kitchen cloth, to chastise me for leaving large pieces of garlic in the paste, but she said nothing. She began frying the onions in Bibi Saffiya's pot in preparation for the meat. And for the servants' pot, I poured in a jug of water to boil for lentils.

We sat in silence in front of the stove. I cleaned the lentils of small stones and debris, throwing them into the fire, while she stirred the meat into the now-browned onions. The smell of burning dung and roasting meat filled the kitchen.

As she stirred the pot, the bluish blood vessel in her right hand protruded through her leathered skin, and her knuckles whitened around the spoon. The scar from an ancient burn resurfaced as her skin tightened.

It was early fall, so the flies had returned. They seemed to disappear when it got extremely hot, but when the weather was pleasant, they were ever present. With her left hand, Bhaggan took the flyswatter from behind her stool and batted a fly that sat on a slice of onion lying on the floor. She missed it.

She continued to stir the pot with meat and mumbled, "Why did you do it?"

"What?" I feigned innocence.

Her lack of anger scared me. If she had shouted, I might have felt more comfortable.

"You know what. Maalik told me."

I remained silent, and she maintained her monotone.

"You know what she would do if she knew it was my son. My Taaj. You have cut off my nose and left me nothing. What can I say to her? 'After all my years of being a loyal servant to you, my son, the son who keeps disappearing, has slept with your daughter. She might have gotten pregnant, but even if she hasn't, who will want to marry her now?' The household with such a respectable reputation for miles is really a house of sin and debauchery. The only consolation for me is that Maalik has decided to take you in. Even my very simple-minded son knows the extent of the damage you have done to the reputation of this house. Even he knows what you did was so evil, so wrong. Even he knows that as a woman you should have protected yourself, but you instead chose to lead my son on. The poor boy must have left in disgust at being enticed to do what only comes naturally to boys of his age. And, to top it all off, I lied to Saffiya about Zakia's nephew because of you."

This part surprised me. Bhaggan never lied intentionally.

"I have incurred the double sin of maligning an innocent man and outright lying. If I'm found out, it will be the end of me in this house. But what do you care?"

I dared not look up.

"And, as a woman, you should have known better. You don't have the urges like boys. You could have controlled yourself. But you didn't, did you? Maalik told me he saw everything from a distance. He saw you pull Taaj toward you, like a bitch in heat."

I shut my eyes tightly and held in my tears. Her anger wounded me deeply, but she wasn't finished. She continued, "I treated you like a daughter. I took care of you. I washed you. I fed you. And this is what you do in return?"

I hadn't thought of her. I had thought only of myself. But how could I think of her and myself at the same time? She was a woman who had lived her life, made her choices. I had to take care of myself. If I didn't, no one else would. Didn't everyone do that? My throat began to tighten, and then I whispered, "I had no choice."

"Choice? It's all already written." Her voice became shrill. "You do what is expected. You take what is given and make the most of it. Who are you to think you will get more than the rest of us? You already have more than your own birth mother could have given you. You think she would have done more than what I or Saffiya has done for you? She left you at your most helpless. Maybe she thought it better that you die than live a life of false hope."

I had cleaned every last stone from the orange lentils. My hands were steady as I placed the dish under the streaming water from the faucet. The lentils, agitated by the water, circled in the dish, creating a foam that I scooped off and threw down the drain.

We continued our work in silence, conscious of each other but choosing to stay disengaged, until she caught my eye and, in a low voice, touched my soul. "You have left me nothing. Nothing. My husband is gone. My son is dead. You took one yesterday, and you're taking the other today." Tears rolled down her cheeks. I had seen her cry, but I had never seen her tears.

What kind of daughter had I been to the only woman who had ever been a true mother to me? I had thought she would be happy that I was marrying her son. Maybe, under different circumstances, but in freeing myself, I had tightened the noose around Bhaggan.

She continued stirring the pot. I got up to get some water to add to the meat.

"And now she wants me to pay for the buffalo. It'll take me years to pay her back. I will be in the kitchen till I die."

Sacrificial Buffalo

The night before my wedding day, Maria and Hamida came to prepare me. Maria rubbed a slimy but fragrant paste of chickpea flour, turmeric, mustard oil, and rosewater on my arms and legs and then on my face to soften my skin. Then Hamida decorated my palms and soles with henna. She covered my nails with henna, too.

They did all this sitting on the charpoy on which we both slept, and sang wedding songs to add to the festivity: "An idiot groom has been bequeathed me."

Hamida sang a traditional wedding song that mocked the groom. She giggled as she applied the cooling henna to my palms. She sang through all the verses, including the one about the groom who brought cauliflower, instead of flowers, and lay under the bed, instead of on top of it. Maria laughed, too, but I couldn't join in. The song that was sung in jest at weddings sounded too close to home. I felt raw with sensitivity. I had never felt so vulnerable, so unsure of myself.

Sultan, Taaj, Maalik—weren't they all the sons of the same father? Wouldn't I find as much happiness, as much love, as much respect with any one of them? Who else would have asked for my hand? The other village boys were all the same.

And Bhaggan was like a mother to me. More than a mother.

She hadn't deserted me. But she wasn't happy with what I had done. How dare she? Wasn't I doing her a favor? I knew how she liked to keep her kitchen. I made her tea the way she liked it, with an extra lump of sugar and the cream off the milk. No one else could serve her better as a daughter-in-law than I could. Her disappointment about my marriage to Maalik was presumptuous. She should be glad that I had agreed.

My shoulders stiffened, and Maria rubbed harder to soften the twitching muscle in my arm. Sensing my stress, she started to sing the mournful tune of one of the more beautiful songs.

"I never argued or quarreled with you, Mother / Hold the palanquin that tears me away from you, Mother."

Tears trailed down their shiny cheeks as Maria sang, but I sat stone-faced, smelling of mustard and roses laced with henna. There would be no bridal palanquin, and I had no brothers to carry me to my husband's home. And now my mother had become my mother-in-law and I wasn't sure that she loved me anymore.

"You're not going to cry tomorrow?" Hamida joked with me. "What kind of bride are you? One who is ready to leave her home as soon as she finds a groom."

I gave a halfhearted smile, but I knew I wouldn't be able to even pretend to cry as I left to be with Maalik in his hovel near the canal in the middle of the cane fields. I didn't feel like talking to either of them.

After the bridal preparations, Hamida left for her parents' home and Maria cuddled up to me. It was the last time my friend would spend the night with me.

For brides in the village, the preparation would last a week, but for me, one night sufficed. Bibi Saffiya didn't care too much for the noise of singing and dancing around the house, so the village women kept their distance.

It had been a few years since Maria and I had last slept on the same charpoy, and I wasn't used to her kicking at night. My sleep was restless, but hers was peaceful. My neck felt stiff from trying to share the pillow with my friend.

I woke to the sound of the maulvi's call for the morning prayer dueling with the wailing of a buffalo. It was my wedding day, and the buffalo would be slaughtered to celebrate my union with Maalik. I lay motionless on the charpoy in the room I shared with Bhaggan, staring at the cobweb on the wooden rafters.

The buffalo had been brought closer to the house, separated from the small herd that belonged to Bibi Saffiya. It had been tied to a stump close to the kitchen and to our bedroom. Maybe it was the separation from the rest or a premonition of its untimely end, but the animal wailed again, and this time Maria woke up and turned over. She looked at me.

"You stay here. I'll bring you your breakfast," she said.

"I'm not hungry," I responded, though I appreciated her concern. But she didn't listen to me and left the room to find some food for me on the morning of my wedding to Maalik.

I lay on my charpoy a little while longer, but, feeling suffocated inside the room, I covered myself with my chador and left to witness the slaughter.

As I walked toward it, the buffalo sensed my company and turned its head in my direction, its deep, almond-shaped eyes looking directly at me. It blinked and swished its tail.

Maalik took great pride in the appearance of all his buffalo, but this one chosen for our wedding, he said, was the most beautiful he had seen. It was one that Saffiya had brought from a seller from the mountains two years before. Since the day it had arrived after its long trip in a truck, Maalik had cared for it as a child, better than a child.

Now, on the day of our wedding, I stood staring at the glorious animal, his blinding albino skin now covered in bright patches of henna and garlands of tinsel and roses to celebrate his glorious end, standing in a fresh pile of dung.

Inside the kitchen, a few steps away, Bhaggan and Maria were preparing breakfast, and here I stood, staring at a living being that would be dead within the hour. It would be sacrificed for a happiness that I didn't believe was mine.

I looked away from the buffalo and noticed Maalik and Hamida's father with a few other village men walking toward me. I pulled the chador more tightly around me, hiding my face. Mesmerized by the buffalo, I turned toward it again.

If my presence had calmed the animal, the sound of the men walking toward him made him bellow again. He began wailing loudly. Maalik sped up and reached the buffalo and began stroking it. The dancing bells that he had tied to its hooves jangled as the buffalo darted frantically. Maalik pulled at the rope with one hand and stroked the animal with the other, making soothing sounds as he did so. The animal's eyes darted as it was led to the sacrificial site near the stream.

Maalik walked with the buffalo, calming it, stroking it with his right hand and feeding it lumps of raw sugar with the left. It was not appeased. And when Hamida's father arrived with the knife, it bellowed in a half-human scream. I stood hypnotized by the terror that my wedding celebration was creating, wanting to look away but not finding the power to do so.

The cow's head bent backward with the first slit, and Hamida's father's face was drenched with blood.

"Bring the towels!" he shouted.

Flies whirled around the fountain of blood. One flew toward me. It landed on my cheek, and I stood motionless. The fly crept up my cheek and looked into my eye. My eyelids half-shut, I stared into the fly's eye. Maintaining visual contact, I thought I saw it wipe the blood splatters from its wing. Both of us blinked, and then the fly ascended.

The blood the fly had brought with it felt warm against my cold skin. I heard Maria call for me, but the slaughtered animal still transfixed me. I stared into its maddened, dying eyes, reminding myself that a slaughtered animal is not a dead animal.

Zakia had taught us this during our lessons about religion. A dead animal cannot be eaten, but the blood of a slaughtered animal is drained, which means it's not really dead. It has served a higher purpose. It has been selfless—a gift for humans, the supreme creation.

Even as a child, I wondered how supreme I was, given that our rankings had to do with things over which we had no control. It mattered if we were of a different sex. It mattered if we knew more or less than others. It mattered if we looked a certain way. But, most of all, it mattered when we were born and to whom.

Animal slaughters were not uncommon in the village, and this was not the first time I had witnessed the spectacle. Maria had often joined her father, Isaac, to clean the blood and gore after a chicken, a goat, or even a buffalo had been sacrificed. Sometimes Maria would be given chicken livers, which we would roast on the coals in Bhaggan's kitchen, but today the scene had sickened me. It had reminded me of what I could not change in my life. My birth had decided my life, and nothing would change its course.

But this was not the day to ponder such thoughts. Maria brought me back to the present. Worried that the putrid smell of fresh dung on my skin would destroy all the hard work from the previous night, she ran toward me, ushering me into the kitchen. I still had to eat my breakfast, and later in the morning I would bathe and dress for the wedding. Hamida had ironed my outfit for me, and the three of us, Maria, Hamida, and I, would lock my shared bedroom door to prepare me for the event.

Oblivious to my stomach churning, Maria tried to force me to have a freshly made paratha and a cup of sweetened, milky tea, but I pushed it away.

"Amman Bhaggan told me to make sure you finish it," she said. "She's worried that her daughter-in-law won't be strong enough for her son on their wedding night," she added.

"Don't talk nonsense," I admonished her, half hoping Bhaggan's concern was true.

Maria knew everything about what had happened between Taaj and me, yet she seemed to think my wedding would give me a fresh start. All I had done earlier would be forgiven, and maybe she was right. I could at least hope she was. I nibbled on the paratha, not wanting to argue with her. I felt my strength being slowly sapped from me, and I figured she was right that some sort of sustenance would renew it.

Amman Bhaggan returned to the kitchen after serving Saffiya her breakfast. She took her place on her *peerhi* by the stove and started cooking parathas for the rest of the staff. As she drizzled ghee on the steaming bread on the darkened *tawa*, she said, "My daughter, eat your breakfast, then help me with the garlic. I have called Hamida and her mother to help with the other work, but I'll need you this morning."

"But it's her wedding day," Maria began to complain.

"That's all right," I interceded. I wanted to peel the garlic. It would make my day return to a normalcy that was familiar and comforting. With my henna-brightened fingertips, I carefully took another piece from the paratha and nibbled on it.

❧

TO CLEAN THE garlic from my hands, I rubbed lemon juice on them before I bathed under the hand pump, and then disappeared into Bhaggan's room to prepare for my wedding in the afternoon.

Maria and Hamida joined me on the charpoy that Maria and I had slept on the night before. Hamida rubbed *chameli* oil on my body to soften it, and Maria combed my hair to help it dry before she braided it.

My wedding outfit, now shaped to my size, with Hamida's mother's help, lay spread out on Bhaggan's charpoy. The armpits were still stained with Saffiya's sweat from when she wore it as a young bride. To hold up my *shalwar*, Maria had threaded into it a bright red, intricately woven cord, Hamida's wedding gift to me. The tassels of the cord were decorated with multicolored beads that would probably not stay on too long.

For my hair, Hamida had made a bright pink cotton braid extender, with gold thread–covered endings, that had already started to unravel.

"Don't worry. I'll fix it," Hamida comforted me. With only a week to make the two items, she had had to cut corners.

Maria forced bright green glass bangles over my hands, oiling them to help push them onto my wrists. Two had broken on her first attempt, leaving a trickle of blood and burning cuts on my right hand.

"I'll put some powder on the cuts to stop the bleeding," said Maria.

"Aren't you happy that you're not marrying that creep?" Hamida said, as she bit off the offending gold thread from the hair extender.

"Can you believe Zakia asked for my hand? And my mother

said she would rather throw me down the well than give me that fate?" she added.

It didn't bother me anymore that someone whom Hamida had turned down had asked for my hand. Of all that had happened to me in the past few weeks, that was the least troubling event.

Not getting an answer from me, Hamida continued, "If you ask me, you'll be happy with Bhaggan as your mother-in-law. She's always treated you like her daughter anyway."

Yes, I consoled myself. *Bhaggan is like a mother to me. She will never let me down.*

"Maalik, on the other hand . . ." Hamida laughed. "I always thought Taaj would marry you. But what do I know?"

She spoke as if someone had been planning my future. But to me, my fate seemed like reactions to my attempts at happiness. My interest in Sultan had led to his death. My enticing Taaj in reaction to the marriage proposal of Zakia's nephew had led to this situation I was still unsure about.

Taaj had not returned after that day I had lain with him. I wondered what he would think when he came home and discovered I'd married Maalik in the time he was away. Maalik seemed happy about the marriage, but Bhaggan was not.

And me? I would move to a hut in the middle of the cane fields and live with Maalik. I knew Bhaggan as a mother, but as a mother-in-law, would she be any different? If I stayed active, took care of the house, I hoped she would come around and be the caring person she had been before all this had happened.

Maria and I focused on the bangles and didn't respond. I felt my face redden, but before Hamida could say anything else, we heard a knock on the door. This startled us both, and Maria swore under her breath as another bangle broke and another thin gash appeared on the back of my thumb.

"Let us in. Maulvi is here for the *nikah*," Bhaggan announced from outside.

Maria got up and unlocked the door, and Hamida covered my head with a chador.

The maulvi entered the room, with Hamida's father, the witness, close behind. Bhaggan stood in the doorway.

Hamida brought in a high stool so that the maulvi could sit next to me. He sat down, read a few verses, and then asked me three times if I would marry Maalik. I bowed my head three times in agreement and then placed a thumbprint on a paper that I couldn't read.

I felt the tender weight of the maulvi's hand on my head as he blessed me. It must have been his wife who had forced him to speak out for her nephew. He bore me no ill will, and I was thankful for that.

Maria put her arm around me, and I sensed her silent sobs. I didn't look up until everyone had left the room, and then I said to Hamida, "Lock the door again, and I'll change now."

Then Maria and Hamida escorted me from my room to a clearing under the *shahtoot* tree, where the wedding feast and festivities would occur.

Some of the village women sat on a charpoy covered with newly washed sheets and a few round cushions. As limited seating for the other villagers standing in the shade of the trees, an assortment of chairs had been brought out from the house, and in front of them two chairs were placed side by side for Maalik and me.

I walked stiffly toward my seat under the trees. My outfit was uncomfortable, and Hamida had pulled my hair too tight when she had made my braid with the extender, which had already started unraveling again. My hand was still cut up from the glass bangles. The black kohl in my eyes had made them water, which Maria interpreted as tears, and I let her believe that.

This was where I had first lain with Taaj, but a group of village women now sat on the charpoy where I had felt as if I had gained so much control. I stared at the women, and they just talked to each other, ignoring me.

I wondered where Taaj was right then. I would be doing with Maalik what I had done with him, but without a frog under my foot. I stifled a nervous giggle at this thought and looked around to see if anyone had seen me smile.

Bhaggan had a strange look on her face that I could not interpret. *Did she see me smile?* I looked at my henna-covered feet again, not sure how to respond to her. I couldn't remember when I had last been so unsure about Bhaggan.

The wedding meal was served. Maalik came and sat next to me, but no one brought us the mirror to gaze at each other.

Hamida pulled off his shoe and then turned up her nose, since it was covered in mud. He gave her a ten-rupee note, and she returned it. There was no laughter, no argument.

For the wedding entertainment, the village women pushed the charpoys to one side and stood them up. One woman stood in the center, and another brought out an empty pitcher, which she would play as a drum with a slipper and her hand.

The women began to chant a familiar phrase, and the woman in the center danced to the beat. I strained to recognize her, but by now I was tired of sitting on the chair for so long without moving. My back hurt, and I yearned for my charpoy.

"Rancid rice and lentils ravaged my liver! Rancid rice and lentils ravaged my liver!" the dancing woman gasped. I knew this routine of singing and dancing from other village weddings and times of celebration, like the birth of a boy.

The women encircling the dancer and the pitcher player

repeated the absurd phrase, clapping in unison, a human drum. Eyes shut, face to the night sky, body arched as if doing the limbo, the dancing woman collapsed in a frenzied heap on her back. The others burst out laughing.

Another dove into the circle, replacing the first as the whirling dervish in the center. As the beat reached a crescendo, the circle of clapping women stepped back. Tearing at her hair and clothes, the woman in the center now chanted, "I crush the white ants that bite me. I crush the white ants that bite me."

I now understood the sexual innuendos in every gesture, and the giggles and guffaws that followed. Some of the women had chosen to dress up for the wedding, but most wore mismatched outfits, as if they had left their homes on the spur of the moment. A few half draped their chadors, revealing multiple layers of earrings in one ear.

My exhaustion escalated as I watched their glass bangles harmonizing to the rhythm of the empty water pitcher, beaten with a broken plastic slipper and a shard of broken pottery. The women relished this mysterious entertainment. Sweating, clapping, thumping, they concluded the performance with a frenzied hilarity, and I waited to be led away to my new home.

TWELVE DEGREES BELOW
THE HORIZON

Rustling Cane

~~~

I look at the stars and I see you," Maalik said the night we moved our charpoys outdoors. In my eighth month of pregnancy, the airless mud hut suffocated me. The smell of cow dung and the fear of wild boar were preferable to our one-room home, ventilated only by the cracks in the wooden door.

The rough rope of the charpoy dug into my left hip bone as I peered into the darkness at Maalik's two dogs, sitting apart and protecting the buffalo, which stood at some distance from our hut, chewing cud. I could understand why Maalik was mesmerized by these animals he cared for. Their slow, hypnotic movements as they ate, as they chewed, and as they blinked their enormous eyes consumed my thoughts.

I slipped into a space inside myself as I felt Maalik's breathing beside me. We had left the other charpoy in the room, so I lay with my back to him while he reclined on the pillow we shared, looking up at the star-filled sky, puffing clouds of bidi smoke toward them.

A mosquito buzzed above my head, and I sensed the quick movement of Maalik's hand silence it. We lay in silence for some time, and then the two dogs lifted their heads and stared into the rustling fields.

Maalik explained sleepily, "That's not a breeze. Those are wild boar nesting their young. On some nights, they peer out of the fields and look at the buffalo, and I see the sparkle in their eyes. But I pick up the gun that Saffiya gave me, and they disappear."

Could boar distinguish between a stick and a rifle? I wondered, but I remained silent, wondering if they chose to listen to our whisperings in the night. A wild boar had bitten off Hajjan's foot many years earlier, before I was born. I imagined the pain that might cause and felt my baby flutter inside me. I rubbed my stomach to calm her down. My heart began thumping, nourishing my fear. I squinted into the darkness of the fields, searching for the shine of a boar's eyes.

My fear reminded me of the night Taaj dared Maria and me to listen to the ghosts of her mother's dead babies at the canal bank. Our own reflections in the dark waters terrified us. At night, the menace of silent shadows, howling hyenas, and wild boar was treacherously magnified, but I buried my panic deep inside.

The dogs placed their heads down again. The danger had passed.

Our bodies touched briefly as Maalik shifted his weight to pull another bidi from his pocket. I was used to his silence during the day, but at night the fumes of his bidi opened his mind and made him talk. He never expected me to respond. He talked and I listened.

"Sultan died and Taaj left, and I sat by myself with the buffalo. On the canal bank, I watched them dip in and out of the water and stared at the sun sinking into the horizon. Fireflies shone over the glistening black buffalo. And I thought of you."

In the past months, I had learned how different Maalik was from my perception of him when we were young. As children, Taaj and I had made fun of him. Laughed when he repeated himself consistently. Ignored him when he talked out of turn.

Now Taaj was gone. He had not returned since the night we had slept together. His memory was blurring because of the memories I was creating with Maalik. I could remember his handsome face and his laugh. Maalik never laughed, and he wasn't as handsome, but his thoughts were deeper. I had never heard anyone talk about the things he discussed. And he never talked about them in the daytime.

But when we lay together at night, he was a different person. He shared his thoughts, sometimes beautiful and sometimes strange. Like his mother, he told stories, but they were different. They were about what he believed had happened in our lives. And they started and ended abruptly, with no connection to each other. I never interrupted or asked questions. He told his stories as if he were talking to himself.

I lay beside him, imagining his world.

"You were like the smoldering sun to others. The sun that killed Sultan and lured Taaj. But for me, you're a star. Just like your name. A star that tells me where to go. The village men and women, they laugh at me. They say you made a fool of me. But I am no fool. They don't know what I know. They didn't see what I see. You needed someone to protect you."

He took a deep puff of his bidi. "Taaj was the fool. You gave yourself to him. Look at what he did. He left you. But I knew better. He pretended he was smarter than I was. He laughed at me. You did, too. But I didn't care. So long as you noticed me. The villagers, they don't realize that's all I need."

Maalik had told me this before. My existence was all he needed. I couldn't understand. Was this love? Did I feel the same way for him?

He became more animated as he spoke. "Tara. Allah is my witness. The stars are my witness. If anything happened to you, I would kill myself. Life without you would be my death."

This took me by surprise. He was professing his love for me, but I felt nothing.

My baby inside me kicked for attention, and I stroked her to calm her down.

"The day we were married, I knew I had caught a star that I could keep. Like the fireflies. But they would die when I clutched them in my fist. Their light dissolved. But you, Tara, my star, you're with me, and you shine."

I stretched my foot to relieve the cramp I felt and thought of the past eight months as his wife, living in the hovel near the cane fields. Every morning I bathed in the canal before the field hands began their work. On the outdoor stove, my kitchen, I made the morning roti and cane-sweetened tea for both of us. I wrapped a piece of mango pickle in a roti for Maalik's afternoon meal when he took the buffalo to water.

Every day I walked the long distance through the fields to Saffiya's house to help Bhaggan prepare the meals of the day and returned before sundown.

Maalik was not a demanding husband. On Eid day, he brought me a pair of green leather slippers with gold embroidery that absorbed the dust from the unpaved paths I walked and became brown. They also became soft, and as I slid my feet into them, I was reminded of the comfort I was becoming accustomed to in my new life. I did a lot of what I had done before I had married Maalik, but now I did not have anyone telling me what to do.

Every day, I cooked meals that I served to others; every other day, I warmed the soap and washed clothes; and once a month, Maria and I made dung cakes to build the fires to cook the meals and warm the soap. But I did this knowing it was what I did well. All the while, my baby was growing inside me.

Maalik and Bhaggan became the two poles of my existence. I started and ended my days with him. I spent the time in between with Bhaggan in Saffiya's kitchen. She seemed to have forgotten her grudge about having to pay for our wedding. What else would she have done but spend her time in the kitchen? That was all she had ever done. She didn't know anything else.

At times the two of them blurred into one: hazel eyes, adoration for the dead and disappeared.

Without a pause, Maalik switched from me to his brothers.

"Sultan was like a god. I remember him so well. Do you remember him? My hair, it's not like his. His was always combed back. Mine curls. What do you think Taaj is doing now? Does he think of us? Amman waits for him to return."

He always became more excited after his second bidi.

"And remember that time in the garden when Taaj said you would marry Sultan? But you didn't. You married me instead. Isaac said we shouldn't break flowers from the garden. Even now, I understand what he says better than anyone else. Better than his daughter. He can't talk, but I know what he's signing."

He placed his hand on his heart and then pointed at me.

"You know what that means? It means I care for you. People think he's not smart because he can't talk. Like me. I talk, but they think I don't know enough. But look. I married you, and we'll have a baby."

I had never known that he was close to Maria's father, Isaac. There were so many things that I had never noticed that Maalik had told me in the past eight months.

As always happened, I was beginning to feel drowsy and drifted into a half sleep. Suddenly, the dogs began barking and I awoke. Maalik was no longer lying beside me. I looked around, but he was gone. I panicked. Where could he have gone at this time of night? Why had he left me alone?

Usually he woke me up before he left to check the buffalo or went to relieve himself, and this bothered me. I had complained to him and told him to let me sleep, rather than announcing his departure. But that didn't stop him from continuing to wake me, so what had happened now? Why had he left without waking me?

I was too scared to go look for him, so I sat upright on the charpoy with my chador wrapped tightly around me. I peered into the night, into the depths of the cane field, hoping to see him appear, and then I heard a crunch behind me.

"What?" he said, as I stared nervously in his direction. "You've told me so many times not to wake you. And now you're upset that I didn't."

He pulled at his clothes, and I realized he had just gone to relieve himself. He lay down beside me, and I settled down, too, placing my hand on his shoulder. His callused hand covered mine as we fell asleep.

THE NEXT MORNING. Bhaggan took me to see the midwife in the next village. The hour-long walk left Bhaggan panting and holding her side. We stopped every ten minutes for her to catch her breath.

"Why, Amman? Have you been staying up at night, praying for Sultan?" I asked her.

She burped loudly. "No, my daughter. I ate the curry that Hamida's mother brought over. It's given me indigestion." But I had seen her with indigestion before. It didn't leave her breathless this way. I wondered if her concern about the debt or Taaj's disappearance had weakened her, but she soon let me know what was troubling her.

"Can you believe her?" she panted, as we walked along the

dusty path. I knew Bhaggan was referring to Saffiya. "She can't find her earrings, and she says Taaj must have taken them when he disappeared."

I reached out for her hand as she stumbled on a rock. I held it tight and said nothing.

I had forgotten about the earrings. Why would Saffiya think of them now, after all this time? She hadn't mentioned them to me when I had placed her ironed clothes in her closet, so why did she need them? It was the month of fasting, and there was no marriage for her to attend where she would need them.

"She says she put them under the Holy Book a month before your wedding. My son might be irresponsible, but he's not a thief. How dare she!" She stopped again and pointed to a nearby small mud boundary wall near the canal. "There," she said. "I need to sit down for a bit."

I followed her to the temporary seat she had found under the neem tree. She was panting more than usual.

"I didn't fast today. I couldn't wake up on time. I hope I'm forgiven." Bhaggan didn't say the five daily prayers, but I had never known her to miss the daylong fasts.

"You didn't fast, did you?" she asked me. "It'll harm the baby."

I shook my head, still thinking about the earrings. I'd forgotten about them because I would never have occasion to wear them. I realized I needed to return them before they created more problems.

I had planned to wear them to the movie theater with Taaj, but so much had happened, and we had never gone. And I had kept them hidden in the corner of my old bedroom that I shared with Bhaggan. I had forgotten to return them. I had no use for them in my new life with Maalik in the cane fields, but

I needed to find a way to put them back before they created more problems.

"Tomorrow I'll go and organize her closet. I'm sure they're where she put them," I consoled Bhaggan.

"Wait till you hear what the midwife says. I'm going to ask her to show you the flower of Maryam, which will calm you during childbirth. I don't want my grandchild to come before his time. And what does Saffiya need the earrings for, anyway? She's close to her time to meet her maker. She'll need only a white sheet to wrap her then. Everything will be left here, the old hag!"

Bhaggan was as convinced that the baby was a boy as I was that she was a girl. I knew I was right, though. She had spoken to me through her movements. She had kicked me gently from within when I had called her by her name: Shahida, the witness.

I had learned the meaning of the male version of the name, Shahid, when studying the Holy Book with Zakia. I liked it. When I told Maalik, he liked it, too.

And now that I was confident I would have a girl of my own, I would call her Shahida. But there was no deterring Bhaggan, and no reason to. Soon enough, Shahida would be with us.

And I knew the birth would be easy. I was strong and had never suffered any illness or injury, and bringing my first baby into the world would not be difficult. I was confident and urged Bhaggan to move a bit faster and get to the midwife's house, which was now just down the road from us.

I decided I'd return the earrings the next day, to reduce Bhaggan's concern and to take the blame off Taaj.

Flower of Maryam

Bhaggan held on to my arm as we entered the courtyard of the midwife's two-bedroom home. She took us into the smaller room, which had one charpoy, a stool, a sack, and a tin box. This was where she saw her clients. As in all other village homes, the corner of the veranda was the kitchen and on the other side of the courtyard was the bathroom.

We crossed the courtyard, our footprints covering the freshly made diagonal broom lines. I imagined that after our baby was born, Maalik and I would make our hovel into a two-room hut with a spacious courtyard like this one.

In one corner of the courtyard was a lemon tree with mint and cilantro around it; in the other corner, a *chameli* tree sprouted buds, even though it was now much cooler.

The midwife sat us both on the charpoy, got us each a cup of sweetened tea and a biscuit, and then told me to lie down.

"My daughter"—Bhaggan paused to catch her breath—"she is young. I told her the flower of Maryam will ease her pain. I said I'd show her how it works."

The midwife straightened her dopatta, walked toward the corner, and pulled a shriveled, clawlike plant from the dusty sack. A ray of light seeped through the one, very high window in the room and reflected off the grayish mass of stems. This was not a flower. I couldn't imagine what magic it would perform.

I lay on the charpoy, and Bhaggan sat hunched near the end of it. From where I lay, I could see the whole courtyard through the door that stood ajar, since the midwife's husband had not yet returned home and her children played in the room next door. It was also the only way the room could stay ventilated.

The midwife checked my pulse as she responded to the skepticism that I made no effort to hide.

"From the time of the prophet, it has performed miracles. Maybe even before that."

She didn't convince me, but I remained silent.

She was perched on a low cane-and-straw stool. Her *kameez* and *shalwar*, made of an expensive material with large red paisleys, added to her aura of confidence and youth. She might have been about ten years older than I was, and I wondered if I would ever dress like her, with a chador that matched the paisleys.

She pulled up my stained and sweaty *kameez*, exposing my stomach, and I wished I had changed into my special outfit before coming. She rubbed some coconut oil on her hands, and the flat gold ring on her left hand began to shine in contrast with her dark skin.

Then she gently massaged my stomach and my baby responded to her touch. I closed my eyes and reached out to find Bhaggan's hand, and it was clammy. The sweat should have died down by now. This worried me, but then the baby kicked and I opened my eyes.

The midwife was composed as she explained to Bhaggan

why she didn't want to use the flower to calm me down that day . "It's too early. She still has a month, and I'll be wasting a very expensive plant."

"And my grandchild—do you think he's not worth it?" Bhaggan responded, wiping the sweat from her brow with her dopatta and still adamant that the baby was a boy. She reached toward the fan on the tin box. It wasn't hot. I couldn't understand why she was sweating. Despite the time we had been at the midwife's house in the village across the canal, Bhaggan's breath seemed to be lagging at the low boundary wall near the bridge.

"My daughter here is worried. I need her to relax. Show her how the flower will stop her pain as my grandchild enters the world, even if it is a month from now." I was grateful that Bhaggan still called me her daughter, not her daughter-in-law, after my wedding.

"She's not ready yet. She still has time. I'll use it when her time is close. It's expensive. It comes all the way from the desert. I give it to women who can't conceive, and two of my clients miraculously conceived because of it. Flowering it now will be such a—"

Bhaggan didn't let the midwife finish her sentence. She undid a knot from the corner of her dopatta, pulled out a bunch of crumpled notes, and threw one on the tin box.

"Here. I can spend anything for my children and grandchildren. Just put the plant in water and show her how it blossoms, to calm her when her time is near." Bhaggan would not be intimidated by the midwife, but the midwife was also Bhaggan's match. Maybe her dealings with so many families gave her the confidence to speak up.

"I tell you, Amman, I don't want it to make her body react too soon," the midwife responded.

"You think I don't know what it takes to have a child? Three of my own, and the last one after his father had died. I know more about childbirth than you do. Two children, you have, and think that's enough. These new ways. Getting an operation."

The midwife seemed slightly put out by Bhaggan's reference to the personal information she had shared the last time we had come, but Bhaggan was unperturbed and continued her rant about the benefits of more children.

"If my man had not died of a snakebite, I would have had more. But you, you've stopped already. Even when you have a husband."

The midwife glanced at me conspiratorially. I wanted to acknowledge this confident woman with a smile, but I knew Amman Bhaggan would be upset at the open disrespect.

Amman Bhaggan was distracted, rubbing her shoulder as if it pained her and breathing deeply. She swelled her nostrils to keep the air flowing smoothly.

When this happened at home, Saffiya would caution her, in a matter-of-fact way, "Bhaggan, your body is asking for a rest from all that weight you carry around."

The midwife pulled my *kameez* over my stomach and wiped her hands with a small towel on the stool, then went to the hand pump in the courtyard to fill a stainless-steel glass with water and brought it to Bhaggan to help calm her down.

"You should have taken a horse carriage today, Amman," the midwife said.

"Yes. I know. She is getting on in years, and the long walk has tired her," I responded, thinking she was considering Bhaggan's breathlessness.

"No. I'm talking about you. You're too far ahead in your pregnancy to travel such distances on foot."

"Not me," I responded. "I'm made like this glass of steel. I won't break, no matter what happens to me."

The midwife stroked my hair. "You're still a child. Your *amman* should have waited to marry you. You have your whole life to bear babies."

The midwife didn't know I had no real mother. I had met her once I knew I was pregnant, when Bhaggan had brought me to her to confirm it. I had been stunned when she had admonished Bhaggan for letting me get pregnant so young. This was the first time I had heard anyone talk this way. Saffiya, Bhaggan, and the villagers all wanted the young village girls to marry as soon as their monthly bleeding started. I wondered if others thought like the midwife.

Her tenderness bruised me. I felt my eyes begin to water, and I shut them again. I didn't know how to react to such consideration.

I could hear Bhaggan's breathing begin to regulate, as if it had just left the wall and was finally catching up with her. I smiled at the image.

"Maybe she's right," Bhaggan conceded. "I should have sent the horse cart to bring the midwife to the hut in the cane fields."

"She's living there all by herself," the midwife said.

"No. My son Maalik . . ." Bhaggan sounded defeated and added, "What can an old woman like me do? She has to live with her husband. And that's where he lives."

"Bring her back to your home for these last weeks. She will need some care and comfort. What will she do if the baby is born and there's no woman to care for her?" Her compassionate tone was like a gentle massage to my soul.

Bhaggan didn't have time to answer. The sound of the children arguing in the room next door interrupted us. A little girl with a bright pink dress and two braids with pink ribbons burst into the room and hid her face in the midwife's lap.

I turned to where she had entered, and a boy not much older than she was stood frowning in the doorway. I could tell he wanted to enter, but his mother's gaze kept him transfixed. "Remember what I've told you," she said.

His tiny fists were clenched in defiance, as he tried not to respond while he was being disciplined in front of us. From where I lay, I looked at him and smiled, recognizing that feeling of daring to resist. Would my daughter be like him or like Maalik? I could tell he was in no mood to smile back at me as he lifted his chest and held his breath to contain his tears of anger.

"You're supposed to take care of your little sister, not fight with her." She gently pushed her daughter's face off her lap and addressed her.

I looked at the girl. She was smiling. Even at such a young age, she had learned how to get her way, to get her mother's sympathy. But the midwife knew her daughter, and her tone changed as she addressed her. "And you. I've told you to listen to your brother. Respect him. Now go. Let me take care of this woman."

"Is her baby coming out?" The girl's voice reminded me of Maria's when I had cared for her at that age, but she was not as innocent. She was trying to charm her mother before she left the room to be with her brother again.

"Not yet," her mother responded. "She has time."

"Are you going to show her the flower magic?" Her daughter smiled. This little girl knew how to win her mother back.

The midwife stroked her daughter's hair and smiled at her. "Go get me the earthen bowl and fill it with water at the pump."

The little girl rushed out, and her brother followed her. He seemed to have forgotten his original anger and wanted to join in on the fun of the magical flower.

This interaction between a mother and her children was entirely different from what I had experienced or seen with Bhaggan or Jannat, but it pleased me. I would admonish my children like this, and then I would hug them and make them laugh, like the two laughing at the hand pump outside.

I could see the children at play from where I lay. The little boy pumped energetically, and his sister stood close to the stream, barely able to hold the bowl as water splashed every-where.

Her brother, noticing it was too heavy for his sister to carry, took the bowl from her hands and brought it to the doorstep. He stood there, knowing not to cross over it into the room where I lay on the charpoy, and his mother took the bowl from him. She placed the shriveled plant into the bowl. Nothing happened.

The midwife sensed my impatience. "It takes time. Keep looking at the plant."

I'm not sure how long it took, but I could hear Bhaggan's heavy breathing in the background as each bud of the flower unfurled, spreading the twig into a fully blossomed plant. I might even have dozed off for a while, but I was awoken by the midwife explaining what had happened.

"You see. The flower will call to your body to open up, to release the new life. The pain will reduce and become a sweet pleasure when you see your baby for the first time." She touched my stomach again and announced, "You see, even your baby has relaxed as you watched the flower bloom."

Was it possible? I wondered. I had seen the buffalo give birth. One had nearly died because its baby got stuck, but I knew I was strong enough to bear that pain. And I trusted the midwife. She knew what she was doing. She had cared for so many other women through childbirth, even had her own beautiful children.

The midwife was now distracted by a fly that had just entered the room and landed on the rim of the bowl.

"The weather gets slightly cooler and these darned flies reappear," she complained.

"Bring me the flyswatter," she told her daughter, who now wanted to please her mother, so she ran to get it, causing a commotion, and the fly disappeared through the window.

It was nearly time for the late-afternoon prayer. Amman Bhaggan clearly wasn't in any shape to walk home, so the midwife told her son to call the horse-cart owner from the house down the street from her. "Tell the driver to make sure his horse is calm. One of my clients and her mother need to return before dark, but he should drive carefully," she instructed him.

As he left, she reminded me, "Please, stay with your *amman* until the baby comes. Someone will notify me when it's your time, but don't go back to the cane fields until the baby is born."

I couldn't imagine returning to sleep in the room I shared with Bhaggan in the bed I shared with Maria. Not now, with my own baby growing inside me.

The call for the late-afternoon prayer reminded me that I would be returning to a familiar pattern of life before the baby came.

The cart driver pulled his cart up to the midwife's front door and helped Bhaggan and me pull ourselves into the back seat.

Bhaggan blessed the cart driver for helping us: "May you have a long life, my son, and many children, especially boys."

We headed back home, clenching each side of the cart with one hand and waving at the midwife's children with the other.

Breaking Fast

ℒℓℓ

We arrived at Saffiya's house on the horse cart when the time for the late-afternoon prayer had nearly ended.

"The late-afternoon prayer time lasts as long as it takes a man to walk six miles until the sun sets," the maulvi had once told Sultan when he was training him to make the call for the five prayers.

That would be just about two hours, I thought, as I sat in the horse cart, waiting to descend. If Bhaggan and I had walked from the midwife's house, we would have taken much longer, we would have been even more exhausted, and it would have been impossible to prepare the meal for Saffiya to break her fast. Plus, she would have been livid.

While the driver calmed his horse to make sure Bhaggan and I could descend from the cart without falling, I noticed Isaac pruning the lemon trees planted in a straight line in the front yard. He turned to greet us with a smile. I looked at him with fresh eyes now that I knew of Maalik's special bond with him. His hair was nearly all white, and he had slowed down, but he still cared for the plants in the vicinity of the house. Saffiya had hired a young man from another village to assist with the heavier work, but that evening, his assistant must have left early, because Isaac was finishing up by himself.

The lemon trees cast an ominous shadow on the *chameli* bushes in front of them.

"Jinn sleep under the trees as the sun begins to set," Bhaggan used to tell Maria and me when we were young. "Stay away from trees in the evenings, in case a jinn enters your body and captures your soul. They can be good or evil, but since you have no way of knowing, it's best just to stay away from them."

As Isaac walked toward us, with the evening shadows of the trees behind him, I wondered if the jinn had begun to settle in for the night. The leaves of the lemon trees moved, and I shivered. A gloom began to descend on me, but I brushed it aside. A rest and a glass of cool water would calm my exhausted mind and body.

As the horse-cart driver helped us dismount, Bhaggan called to Isaac to bring Maria to the house. He gestured in agreement, returning his clippers to the wooden toolbox near the house, before walking toward his home to call his daughter. His eyes sparkled as he smiled at me, and he touched his stomach and then raised his hand to acknowledge my pregnancy and wish me well. I appreciated the stability Isaac created in our otherwise tumultuous lives.

When I was younger, I had wondered why he couldn't speak. Had something happened before he was born, or had coming into the world silenced him? But he seemed content in his silence.

As Bhaggan and I walked toward her room, I stared after Isaac's upright figure, wearing a wrinkled, graying cotton *kameez* and a brown sarong wrapped around darkened calves. The hennaed soles of his feet were visible with every step he took toward his home.

Maybe his silence gave him the power to stoically endure

an ailing, bad-tempered wife, an invalid daughter, and dead babies.

Bhaggan stumbled toward her room, rather than toward the kitchen, and as she did so, she addressed me: "Maria can help you with the evening meal tonight. I need to straighten my back." Her darkened fingernails dug into my shoulder as she tried to straighten herself.

She staggered to her charpoy. It worried me that, despite the horse cart, she hadn't recovered from her earlier breathlessness. When I asked her if she was all right, she gestured with a flip of her hand for me to go to the kitchen. Bhaggan was always in control, and I was confident that she'd be fine after a rest.

Bhaggan never held back when she was unwell. She was always quick to recover, but when she was sick, she made sure she checked with Saffiya about herbal cures and had even gone to the local dispensary a few times when she'd had severe back pain a few years before. An energizing drip had helped her make a quick recovery. She would tell me if she needed anything. I knew her.

The trip to the midwife had tired me, too, but the sun was beginning to set and it would soon be time for the evening prayer. During the fasting month, this time of day seemed slowed down, but it always accelerated for me if I was in the kitchen. I was relieved that Saffiya was the only one fasting that day. Otherwise, I would have been expected to prepare a feast. I had a few extra minutes to help Bhaggan get settled in her room before I rushed to the kitchen, and for that I was grateful.

As I entered her room, I turned on the solitary bulb. The sun had nearly set, and the one small window in Bhaggan's room didn't provide much light or fresh air. I left a glass of water below her charpoy. She sipped it noisily, spilling some on her chin. I wiped it away with my dopatta, and she mumbled.

"When Isaac returns with Maria, tell him to go to the cane fields and let Maalik know that you're staying with me tonight." And then, in her routine, she made sure I remembered her other two sons: "May Sultan be in Paradise by now, and may Taaj find his way home."

The words were hopeful, but her demeanor was not. A melancholic aura began to descend, and her tone lacked its usual optimism. Could she really still be so exhausted from the walk—or was it that I was in a funk? I needed Maria's company to brighten up the evening.

I resolved to pull the earrings from Sultan's old tin box the very next day. It had been nearly a year since I'd hidden them. I'd return them to Saffiya's closet and put her at ease, and in doing so end Bhaggan's harassment.

"Remember to give Isaac his evening meal," Bhaggan said, turning to the practicalities she was known for handling so adeptly. "I know he's not fasting, but he never eats much anyway."

I walked toward her bedroom door and heard the charpoy creak as she lay back again. I turned to see if she was all right. With great effort, she struggled to turn herself toward the window, away from me, and whispered, "My daughter, turn off the light. I don't think I'll need it anymore."

I looked longingly at my charpoy in the other corner but reminded myself that I would be able to rest as soon as I had finished the last chores of the day.

As I left the room, it was nearly time for the fourth prayer of the day, the prayer to open the fast. And not long after that, it would be time for the final prayer, the time after the red thread of sunset disappeared. I'd learned Sultan's lessons well, I thought, and smiled.

For Saffiya, I would set out a tray with dates and sweetened milk with rosewater. She'd then say her evening prayer, and soon after I would serve the evening meal. The house was eerily quiet, and I awaited Maria's chatter.

During the month of fasting, Saffiya was adamant that all her employees break the daylong fast from her kitchen. It added to the blessings she would receive, and it was a tradition that her father had maintained and that she chose to continue. Every Thursday of that month, Saffiya got Bhaggan to prepare a feast of two large cauldrons of rice and chicken for the whole village. Some Thursdays, she made halvah, too. The village women joined the preparation, and Bhaggan relished the power of having a team at her beck and call to make an indisputably sumptuous feast. There were still three days until Thursday. Bhaggan would no doubt recover by then.

When I heard the maulvi's call for the evening prayer, I rushed to Saffiya's room with the tray of dates and rosewater milk. I was again relieved that Saffiya was the only one who needed a meal that night. I stood by her side while she recited the prayer, before gulping down the milk.

With a thin line of milk covering her upper lip, she said, "You're here late. How will you get back tonight?"

Saffiya had gotten used to my returning to my hut in the cane fields, even though she wasn't happy that no one was around to give her a late-evening massage. Bhaggan was too old and tired, and Maria had to return home to care for her mother.

"The midwife told me to stay here till my time," I responded.

"Good," she replied. "Then tonight, after the evening meal, you can massage my shoulders. I can never convince Amman

Bhaggan to do it. She never has enough energy to care for me anymore."

This annoyed me, but I had learned to hide my feelings from Saffiya. I had planned to spend some time catching up with my old friend, but I would have to massage her, as she expected.

Every day since my marriage, I'd come to wash the clothes and prepare the meal for the day. Maria would join me for a short while. She couldn't stay away from the house for very long, since Jannat's health was failing. Instead of Jannat, Maria now cleaned the whole house. Her mother was too frail to handle the bamboo broom and mop and bucket.

Tonight, when I returned to the kitchen to prepare the evening meal, Maria was already building the fire to warm the food. Bhaggan had cooked it before she'd left the house that morning, and now I took the dough out of the refrigerator and walked slowly toward the stove to join my friend.

"Are you crazy?" she said to me when I sat down beside her.

I looked at her questioningly.

"Have you seen your face? You're exhausted." Maria took the dough from my hands and began to break off pieces and roll them into balls to make into roti.

We both knew that Saffiya would not be happy that Maria was cooking her meals and making her roti, but neither of us cared. I was glad to take a break. I sat on the low stool next to her, leaning against the wall and looking at my feet, which had doubled in size through exertion that day. The warm smell of cooking roti comforted me. Sparks flew playfully around the stove, and I was reminded of our childhood, though our roles were now reversed. I talked, and Maria listened to my recollections of the day. I told her about the midwife and her children and how they played together, and about the flower of Maryam and its magical power to relieve the pain of childbirth. When I told her how it had relaxed me, Maria smiled at my happiness.

"What about you, Maria? How is your mother doing? You never tell me about her. Does Stella ever come to visit?"

"Stella is working in the hospital. She helps with the patients," she said, as she expertly flipped a roti onto the open fire. It filled with hot air that swelled it into a ball.

"The nuns taught her how to read and write, so they gave her a job." So Stella had found her way. Maria told me about her mother, too. "The nuns send us money and medicine. When I took her to see the doctor, she said Amman will probably not live to an old age. They told me to keep her as happy as I can."

She didn't cry as she told me this. My little friend had matured.

While we talked, she prepared the meal for everyone. She wrapped some spicy potatoes in a roti and covered it with an old newspaper for Isaac and herself. She wasn't planning to eat with me.

"I'll take this home for Abba. He stayed with Amman while I came to help you. You take this tray in for Saffiya, and I'll make another one for Bhaggan. When they're finished, leave everything in the sink, and I'll come in tomorrow morning and wash all the dishes. There's no need for you to tire yourself today."

Maria was the same caring person as always, and even more so, but I didn't want her to think that my pregnancy had weakened me, so I said, "I'll wash them before sunrise, when I wake up to make Saffiya's fasting meal."

She smiled, wiped her hands with her dopatta, and left

with her packaged food under her arm, and I took Saffiya's tray into her room.

Saffiya wiped her face with her cupped hands as she ended the evening prayer. She stepped off the prayer mat, folded it, then addressed me. "Did you eat already? I hope you're not fasting at this late stage of pregnancy."

I was glad she had some concern for me. "Bibi, I'll eat before I take Bhaggan her meal. I'm not hungry yet."

"Then sit for a while, and I'll finish my meal. I've had a terrible headache all day because of my fast. May Allah forgive me. I don't want to diminish all the blessings I've earned by complaining, but I can barely think straight. I've always suffered this way. You remember before your wedding, I was so stressed. Blinding headaches. They've tortured me since I was a child. Bhaggan knows. She's the one who massaged my head even when I was young."

I wasn't used to her engaging me in conversation. It was as if I were replacing Bhaggan.

"Today Amman Bhaggan is exhausted," I shared. "The walk to the midwife's house tired her."

"What did she say, the midwife?" Saffiya seemed interested. Considering she had never borne a child, I wondered what she thought of my pregnancy.

"She told me not to go to the cane field and to stay at home until it was time, and then I should send for her."

And then I told her about the flower.

"Yes," she said. "My father showed me the flower when I was very young. It is hypnotic—so much power."

"Amman Bhaggan paid ten rupees for the flower and then another ten for the trip on the horse cart."

"Your *amman* is spending a lot on you." Saffiya laughed.

Was she making fun of Amman Bhaggan? I was enraged

and didn't have the sense to hide it, and blurted out, "I don't even know if she's finished paying for the buffalo." And then I added what I knew about the money Bhaggan said her husband had given Saffiya as a payment for land the day he died. "And she says her husband gave you some money but she never got anything for it."

Saffiya's tone became cold, and she stopped chewing her food. She raised an eyebrow and glared at me. "What else has she told you?"

I had abandoned all fear, but now my heart began to pound as I explained what I knew.

"She told me that her husband gave you all their savings the day he died of a snakebite, and you gave her nothing in return."

She finished chewing her morsel and then spoke slowly, enunciating each word. "You listen to me. Amman Bhaggan chose to stay with me. I haven't forced her. Her husband was in debt. Debt that you can't even imagine. I know she says he was smart, like Sultan, but he was a fool, just like Sultan, but even more so because he lived long enough to burden Bhaggan with three children and nothing to pay for them."

She was looking directly at me, and I began to feel weak, but she wasn't finished. "And he took his own life. And Bhaggan knows that. He had told her so many times that he would drown himself, and he did."

I knew the enormity of taking one's own life meant no burial space in the graveyard, the whole family slandered.

She continued, "I paid the old snake charmer to find a snakebite. Bhaggan knows this, but she creates memories."

She told me how she had paid Bhaggan's husband's debts and had kept all the creditors at bay. I was surprised that she wasn't angry with me. She told me that she had also paid for the buffalo, and I wondered why Bhaggan had never told me all this. If she thought of me as her daughter, why had she not thought of sharing this with me?

"You know what they would have done to a young woman and three children? The brick kilns are full of indentured slaves, whole families of debtors. But your *amman* got a home, and I gave it to her."

She sipped the water, rinsed her mouth, and spat into her spittoon.

The room around me began to spin. I had not eaten, and I was still exhausted. I leaned on the wall, hoping to be able to stand. I needed to get to my room and lie down.

Saffiya looked at me, and I saw a look of concern that I had never seen before pass across her face.

"I should have kept those thoughts to myself, but I know you are too smart. And I also know that Bhaggan is like a mother to you."

Yes, I thought, more than anyone else, Bhaggan had cared for me.

"Her parents made a bad marriage arrangement for her and then wanted nothing to do with her. Her husband's family was worse. After his death, they didn't want to be burdened with a young widow and three children, along with all the debt they had inherited, so they packed up and left the village without telling anyone."

Did Bhaggan think I would judge her husband's actions like the villagers had? My own mother had deserted me at my most vulnerable. If she had shared this with me, we would have gotten closer. I thought her parents had loved her, supported her. I had grown up thinking that I was the only one devoid of parental love.

And her husband had chosen a more final way out of her life.

Just like Taaj, I thought. *That's what Bhaggan must have feared—that her son was now like his father and the family that deserted her.*

Saffiya continued clarifying her perspective on Bhaggan's life: "Her sons are no better. The only one who had a bit of intelligence turned out to be a thief."

I clenched my fists as I heard this. I had to clear Taaj's name, if not for him, then for Bhaggan. I had to prove that Taaj was not a thief. I forgot my exhaustion and decided to fix the situation right then and there.

Saffiya finished her meal and got up from her charpoy to prepare for the night prayer, which followed very quickly after the evening one. I would use this opportunity to replace the earrings, but I needed to be cautious.

I gathered the dishes in the tray and carried it to the kitchen. My baby moved inside me, and I rubbed my stomach to put her at ease. She must be hungry, but I would take care of her later. First, I needed to fix the problem I had created.

Saffiya would spend some time in the bathroom doing ablutions to prepare for the night prayer. I would rush back to Bhaggan's room, find the earrings, and return them before she began the last prayers of the day.

I left the door to Bhaggan's room ajar, and a stream of light from the rising moon cut through the shadows inside. I didn't want to wake Bhaggan, but she mumbled something when I entered.

"What, Amman?" I asked.

"Sultan, my son, you look good," she said. I figured she must be dreaming. "Your brother Taaj is still as naughty as he was when he was young. He stays hidden when he's in trouble."

How often did she meet with Sultan in her dreams? I tried

not to wake her while I fumbled around in Sultan's tin box under my old bed. I could feel the buttons on his outfit folded neatly inside. As I scraped my hand on the bottom of the box, I felt a few pens and pencils and two books.

My baby kicked me, wanting me to straighten up and give her more space, but I stayed hunched, looking for those earrings. I pulled at the box and pushed my hand farther back until I felt the hook of one earring. The other had gotten separated, and it took me a few more minutes to find it.

"Who is it?" Amman Bhaggan had woken up.

"Me, Amman. I'll be back with your meal just now." I thought this would be enough to calm her.

"Just a piece of roti and some tea, nothing else," she said. But then she asked, "Why are you down there?"

I stood up, holding the earrings tight in my right fist. I chose not to move the box back under the bed, to avoid Bhaggan's suspicion. I would return it when she wouldn't notice.

"I'll be right back," I said, and I rushed out of the room.

When I returned to Saffiya's room, I was relieved to hear water splashing in the bathroom. She was still preparing for her prayers. I pulled her keys from under her pillow, but just then the bathroom door opened.

"Pass me the prayer mat," she said, wrapping her dopatta around her and tightening it to keep her hair securely hidden.

I had the earrings in one hand and the keys in the other, keeping both fists closed. Very deftly, I managed to push the prayer mat in her direction.

As I turned, she stood on the mat, and that was when I decided I'd have to return the earrings while she was in the room. I knew she would be looking at the prayer mat while she prayed, so I announced flippantly, "Your cupboard lock seems to be open." Even though she rarely left her room, she never left her cupboard unlocked. "I'll lock it before I leave for the night."

With my right hand, I opened the lock with the key, slid the earrings under a pile of clothes, then locked the door. Before I left, I placed the keys back under the pillow as if I were straightening the bed and returned to the kitchen.

I had done it. The next morning, when Saffiya pulled out her clothes, she would see the earrings and would no longer be able to blame Taaj for stealing from her.

My accomplishment revitalized me. The palpitations of my heart energized me to do the one last thing for the day: take Bhaggan her tea with half a roti, on which I would spread some butter and sprinkle some of Bhaggan's favorite sugar.

As I sat down at the stove to make her tea, I felt some moisture in my *shalwar*. In my pregnancy, my body was no longer fully my own. Things that I could not explain happened to it. My feet swelled, my breasts got larger, my hair grew more than it ever had before. The moisture was probably part of the same changes, and anyway, my due date was a month away. I had just this one last thing to do, and then I would be able to lie down and rest.

As I walked toward Bhaggan's room with the tea in one hand, I realized I had left her door ajar when I'd taken the earrings. I hoped no night animal, like a field rat, had strayed into the room. They terrified me. But this wasn't the season for them, and I couldn't hear any scuttling. It was a still night. Even the hyenas were quiet.

I pushed open the door a bit more to make room for my baby to enter, and I smiled to myself. Everyone would spoil this baby: Bhaggan, Maria, Maalik, and most of all, me. I didn't have too much hope about Bibi Saffiya's caring for her, but the love she got would be more than what anyone else I knew had.

The moon was now very bright, and I was afraid that Bhaggan would complain about it. I looked up, surprised at the stillness of the room. No field rats, no snoring, no heavy breathing. My hand went limp, and the tea scalded my arm as the cup shattered on the floor. Still no noise.

Bhaggan's hazel eyes were open, and they stayed open. She was looking directly through me. I tripped on the corner of Sultan's tin box as I moved toward her bed. The noise was jarring, but the sharp pain on my shin made me cry out. As I straightened myself, Bhaggan lay in the same position, eyes unblinking, staring through me. In disbelief, I moved closer, to touch her. To wake her up, even if it angered her. Her hand was still warm, but I knew she would never wake.

I couldn't breathe. I couldn't feel. I couldn't scream.

I turned toward the door. In front of the house, the moonlight created a path toward the fields. That was where I would go. I didn't care how long it would take, but I would find Maalik. I had to tell him what had happened. He would know what to do.

Birth Canal

T he moon had turned a pale yellow as it began to set on the horizon. I couldn't tell how long I had been walking, but I had still only reached the canal bank.

"During a full moon, babies are born before their time," Bhaggan had said to the midwife earlier that day. Bhaggan was aware of the seasons and the movements of the heavens, but to me they were a backdrop with no direct impact on my life. Bhaggan's experiences took on a new meaning for me now that she was dead. It was as if she spoke from above, was guiding me toward the cane field. Or was I imagining it? My back pain was testimony to the truth she spoke.

I should have listened to her. Remembered her wisdom before leaving the house.

Why had I forgotten myself upon seeing Bhaggan's lifeless body? Yes, I needed to get to Maalik, but surely he wouldn't want me walking all this distance in the dark. I should have thought of my daughter. What would happen if my time came now, out here with no one to help me? With no one to care for her? I had made a choice that would leave my own daughter in the same precarious situation in which I had begun my life.

The hyenas were no longer quiet. I heard a dog bark, responding to their howls. The path in front of me was darkening, and I could no longer tell where I was going. I followed the hyenas' mourning howls, knowing that the barking dogs meant that Maalik was close by. I stumbled down the path that led to the cane fields. I forgot the pain of my swollen feet. I ignored the liquid creating a trail behind me.

"Unclean water will leave your body and create a passage for your baby," the midwife had explained to me. Did that mean the baby would be here sooner than I expected? Before my baby was born, I needed to find Maalik. He needed to know about his mother.

But how would I tell him? Bhaggan had made the long journey to the midwife's house to prepare for my childbirth. She had cared for me as even my own mother hadn't. And I had let her die alone. I should have stayed with her when she was calling out to Sultan in her sleep. I should have held her hand and comforted her, let her know how much she meant to me. But now she was gone.

I had prided myself on never crying. Now, when I needed to so badly, my tears remained inside me. I had trained my body not to react, and now it was doing what it had learned.

Maalik would understand. It was nighttime. He would have had his bidi. He would know what I was feeling. I knew it, but I needed to get to him, and I kept stumbling, and my baby kept kicking, excited about the activity at a time when I was usually fast asleep.

As I stumbled toward the fields, I felt a dull pain in my back. My shallow breathing made my head spin. I stopped and sat on a tree stump to try to catch my breath. I felt a dry heave wrench my body, but nothing came out. I had not eaten since I had had the biscuit with tea that the midwife had served us earlier that day. I stared at my swollen feet, now muddied by the liquid leaving my body and the dust from the path. I breathed deeply three, four times. I looked up at the night sky. The moon was disappearing, replaced with a universe of stars.

Was Bhaggan now up in the heavens? Could I make her out in the stars above? I imagined her caring for me, even as she was no longer on this earth. I felt her warmth as a protection around me. A gnawing fear began nibbling inside me, but her memory calmed me and gave me the power to move on.

I reminded myself to breathe deeply before my insides took control of my body again. My back pain became less intense. I focused on the brightest star in the sky.

Maalik had called me his star. Was I that one? Or the smaller one next to it that kept disappearing?

I needed to get back up and find Maalik. I imagined him on the charpoy we shared at night. It was a cool night, but he would have stayed outside. He would be listening to hyenas and wondering why they were howling.

I could hear the dogs, too. Where were they? What had happened to cause such a commotion?

I pulled myself off the stump and began walking toward the canal. A few fireflies were still dancing on the water. How long would they live? They died when their light went out.

My backache returned, this time more intense. Heavier. It was as if my baby were pushing against my stomach with her feet and leaning heavily against my back. My breathing became shallow again. The dry heaving returned. I needed to call out for Maalik, for anyone, to come. My voice would travel at this time of night, but I couldn't bring myself to call out.

I was now crossing the canal and could hear the hyenas. They were calling from the cane fields. What had happened that they wouldn't stop calling? My fear began reaching for my heart. It was now feasting on my insides. It began to suffocate me, and I covered my mouth with my dopatta to keep my breath from escaping. I needed to move on and not let the fear paralyze me.

My eyes strained as I peered into the darkness in front of me. Shadows moved, even though the night was still. I tripped over a rock and steadied myself. I was halfway between Saffiya's house and our hovel. Would anyone find me before it was too late?

A thin mist descended on the canal. From the fields, a rat-like animal scuttled in front of me and jumped into the water. What could have terrified it so to make it take its own life by drowning? What was hiding low in the fields? Was it someone crouching, concealing itself from the hyenas? Or was there something more ominous? The unimaginable jinn of the night? I squeezed my eyes shut and recited the prayers I had memorized under Zakia's tutelage.

The memory of Zakia angered me. I thought of Bhaggan again, but now I found no comfort. Was her spirit following me? Had I created such pain and anguish for her that she would haunt me for the rest of my life? Would my prayers reach her spirit? Would she be with me during the challenge? Hurriedly, I looked behind me, but could see only a darkened blur in the distance. Saffiya's house. My home.

I no longer had control over my body. My fear was suffocating me and pushing my insides out. The midwife had said I shouldn't walk long distances. She had said I should stay with Saffiya until the baby came. I should have listened to her. I should have stayed home. I should have called on Bibi Saffiya when I found Bhaggan. She would have taken care of everything, like she always did.

My baby was ready to come before I was prepared for her.

She didn't care. My legs could no longer hold up my body, and I collapsed on the canal bank. I clawed at a clump of grass, anything to steady me. But the pain consumed me.

I lay back on the bank as the pain subsided. I fumbled to open the string that kept my *shalwar* up and surrendered myself to what was happening.

The pain returned in phases, each more excruciating than the previous. Never before had I experienced such bodily torture. How would I survive it? It had such power that it had taken over my mind.

I shut my eyes and imagined the Maryam flower. When the pain subsided for a while, I thought the magic of the memory might be working. But then it returned, even stronger. How had Bhaggan endured this time after time? The calm and confident midwife, with her loving children—she had gone through this, too. I couldn't imagine how they had continued their lives after enduring the agony. I pushed to end it.

And then an ecstasy enveloped me like a cloud and I gave in to it. I felt my baby exit my body. I heard a whimper, like a kitten, and then a loud, angry cry.

I had survived. I pulled myself up to a sitting position and saw a small, bloodied body lying between my legs. Her dark hair was plastered to her skull. And then she opened her hazel eyes and looked into mine. A teardrop trickled down my cheek.

I took my dopatta and wiped her. She was still attached to me, and I didn't know how I would cut the cord, but I held her to my chest and she suckled my breast.

When I lay back with her, my whole being filled with a peacefulness I could have only dreamed about. My body kept depositing liquids, and I now felt light-headed and delirious and drifted into blissful sleep, choosing to ignore, for now, the dangers around and within me.

THE RED THREAD DISAPPEARS

Witness

e, the flies, were witness three times. We witnessed Tara's desertion, and her death, and her rebirth through her daughter, Shahida.

On the train all those years ago. Her mother, dressed in a black burka, sat on the train, holding her baby close to her. She scanned the station platform from the window. We distracted her by hovering nearby and wanted her to look down at her baby on her lap. She brushed us aside with the corner of her burka. She leaned over Tara, searching the deep crowds, waiting for someone. Two women walked toward her railway carriage, but she was not waiting for them.

A whistle blew, and the train engine shunted, as if to begin its departure. Tara's mother saw someone in the crowd. This excited her. She waved from the window. She shouted. The baby looked up at her. Her mother had young hands, not yet scarred by years of kitchen work. Still soft like a child's, like the hands of the baby she held. The dirt-encrusted fingernails were bitten to the quick. No rings on her fingers, nor gold wedding bangles.

The young mother waved and shouted again. Then she looked down at Baby Tara and placed her on the seat. She would come back; we could tell. She wanted the person she was calling to join her.

Two women entered the carriage. One was dressed in expensive clothes, and the other looked like her maidservant. And then the train started to move and Tara's mother never returned. The women looked in our direction as we covered Tara, protecting her from the evil eyes of the passersby.

The women came close and swatted at us. They picked up the baby and gave her a piece of raw sugar to suck. The train moved faster, leaving the station, and from the window we saw the burka-clad figure, Tara's mother, rush toward the carriage. She never made it, and her screams were muffled by the shrieks of the train picking up speed as it left the station and sped toward the countryside.

We witnessed Bhaggan and Saffiya rescuing Tara and naming her. We witnessed all of Tara's short life.

We witnessed her death, and the birth of her daughter, Shahida, herself a witness to her mother's death. But Tara never realized we were there for her. Her daughter knew from before she was born that we would protect her for all eternity.

Shahida, Tara's only daughter, was born of two fathers at the canal bank. And then a third, the maulvi, came to love her like his own.

We saw what happened that night when Tara drifted into the eternal sleep of ecstasy after the baby came. Never knowing that her husband, Maalik, lay broken at the edge of the fields, having endured his own trauma concurrently with hers.

While Tara staggered toward the cane fields to tell her husband about Bhaggan, we observed Maalik on his charpoy near his hovel from all around—from our lowly perch on a dung pile near the buffalo, and from the heights of the neem trees planted to shade them in the summer heat.

Maalik reacted to the howls of his two guard dogs and walked toward them. One lay near the border of the fields, and the other hovered around. They beckoned Maalik to help, but he didn't know which direction to go in. Hyenas had begun their night call, too.

Somewhere between his dreams and the reality of the night, Maalik walked toward the edge of the fields. He knew something was amiss, but he didn't know what. He would never have imagined that his wife would not return that night. He assumed she was safe in Saffiya's house. He figured the dogs were barking to alert him that he needed to protect the buffalo. Tara would be sleeping in the same room as his mother, as she had done until a year earlier, when she had joined him in the hovel in the cane fields. She would eat a meal cooked by his loving mother. His baby would be safe with her.

He didn't care whether or not the baby was his. He had a family. He had never thought he would be so lucky as to have Tara as his wife. She had wanted Sultan, and then she had slept with Taaj. His brother could have had her forever, but he had left, and Maalik now had a life he could never have imagined for himself. He recalled that early morning when he'd hidden behind the bushes to watch Sultan pinning the *chameli* garlands to Tara's luscious braid, which swung erotically when she went to the hand pump every morning.

Lost in the pleasure of his memories, Maalik picked up his gun and walked away from the buffalo toward the dogs. He entered farther into the darkness and saw a pair of beady eyes glinting from the fields. He pulled his gun closer to his side and moved toward the dogs. A baby boar lay next to his dog. It must have been pulled from its nest in the field. Its mother's eyes glistened from beyond, and the cane around her stirred as she waited—for retribution for those responsible for killing her young.

Maalik looked at his faithful surviving dog and then at the

one that the mother had attacked. The hyenas' howls became louder. They smelled blood and were waiting for more. Maalik knew he would not be able to outrun the boar. He'd never shot the gun and wasn't even sure how it worked. He had never thought he'd have to use it, and now he needed to protect himself and his dog.

We witnessed the horrific eruption of a mother's fury and the helplessness of a man and a dog facing that rage. We watched the foolhardy loyalty of a dog for its master, and the disadvantages of a man with a gun that he had never learned to shoot. We watched the orgy of blood and guts as the hyena orchestra played in celebration of the feast that awaited them.

We, the flies, the witnesses, observed the beloved of Tara lying near the buffalo chewing their cud, oblivious to the severity of their owner's condition. We flew toward him to see if he still breathed. He was covered in blood. His life had been spared, but the horror of having been mauled by a boar emanated from his wide-open, hazel eyes. He had seen and experienced terror that erased all his loving memories of Bhaggan, Tara, and the baby whose birth he was awaiting.

Entranced

W e, the flies, witness to Tara's death, protected Shahida, her daughter, until sunrise. Tara lay on the canal bank where she had given birth to her baby, and the baby lay beside her, covered by her mother's dopatta. One after another, we flies joined to protect the baby.

The dawn sunlight reflected in the dead mother's eyes, searching for the song of lost love.

Love will survive, but I will drown.

It came from a radio hanging from the handle of the milkman's bicycle. The unoiled bike's squeals competed with the blaring music. The bicycle was barely balanced between two large milk cans that wobbled as the milkman tried to avoid the last of the night's hyenas crossing the road and disappearing into the cane fields.

On the road that Tara had walked the night before, two figures traveled in opposite directions. The milkman, on his bicycle, rode toward the village. The maulvi, after making the call for the early-morning prayers, was walking hurriedly toward the main road. He would take the bus to the shrine. The morning sun shone directly into the maulvi's eyes, blinding him in the moment when he turned the corner to face the milkman.

From our perch, we could see the road, but to protect her, we flew over to Baby Shahida, her hand still covered in fluids of her afterbirth, her eyes blinking at the morning star as it faded in the sunlight. She called out to it.

"Who's there?" the milkman shouted.

The milkman and the maulvi heard the baby's cry at the point where their paths met.

The milkman swerved left and then right to balance the two sloshing milk cans. He wobbled for a second and then landed on his right knee, tearing his *shalwar* and losing the top layer of knee skin. He was too distracted to notice the watery milk turning a light shade of pink and then a sloshy brown as it mixed with the blood and then with the surrounding mud.

"Son of an owl! Bastard! Sister fucker!" the milkman shouted.

But the maulvi was already climbing up the canal bank, following the sound, a whimper—a baby?

And then there was silence.

The milkman followed the maulvi up the embankment. He was a crude man made cruder in his pain. He shouted to the maulvi, "Your mother's milk is all over the road. Will she re-place it, or will your wife?"

The sun lifted itself from behind the mist-laden canal just enough for both of them to see the bloodied bodies.

We, the flies, disentangled ourselves from the bodies and disappeared behind the bushes.

Both men looked disbelievingly at what lay before them: Tara dead, and her baby still sucking at her mother, while we protected them both.

For that moment, the milkman forgot his pain and cussed as he exulted in what he saw: "Your mother—it's a miracle! The baby was born of a dead woman."

The maulvi, seeing the truth of what lay before him, shouted back, "Son of an owl! Run to the village and call for help. Tell Bibi Saffiya that Tara is dead and the baby is alive! Go now!"

The milkman nearly rolled down the embankment and rode in the direction of the village.

The maulvi sat down next to Tara and placed his hand on her face. His body shuddered with mournful, soundless sobs.

After a while, we flew toward him and landed on his hand. He looked up at us and thrust us away, so we flew back onto the baby, who had now begun to whimper.

The maulvi then turned around to pick up the baby. He had seen new babies before, but only those who'd been cleaned and wrapped tightly in a sheet. How he'd longed for a baby all these years, and Zakia had had only miscarriage after miscarriage.

The fifth time she got pregnant, the baby stayed for eight months in the comfort of the mother's womb, and then he took his wife, Zakia, to the hospital for a cesarean. The baby never returned home with Zakia.

To Zakia, the maulvi said, "It's the will of Allah."

After that, the maulvi's mother tried to find him another wife. But each time she mentioned it, he looked at her in disgust, and, knowing her eldest son, she backed off.

Then Zakia, broken, suggested another wife, too, and he threw the dinner tray across the room, not caring that the *aloo baingan* splattered everywhere. He left and didn't return for two weeks.

Zakia cleaned the bits of potato and eggplant strewn all over the floor after he left, but the stain remained on the wall and she lay staring at it in the afternoons, somewhere between sleep and wakefulness. If she looked at it from a distance, it looked like a mustache, but if she looked more closely, it looked like the name of Allah. It even had the small connector on top, which in the loneliness of the afternoon was a stronger message that she was not alone. A more powerful being was giving her peace, telling her to stay silent during this ordeal. To keep praying five times a day, and then to add more time during each prayer, and then to wake up before the morning prayer to pray before the prayers of others could be heard.

For two weeks, Zakia prayed for her husband to return, and she made a deal that if he returned, she would stay silent and would not ask for more.

For those two weeks, we witnessed the maulvi sitting at the shrine, praying for peace. Praying for patience. Most of all, he prayed for a baby, in whatever form that might come in. It needn't be his own. It could be a child of the village. He would no longer settle for a child of his own but would become a father to all children. Even if they had their own fathers, he would care for them and then add a layer of comfort to protect them further. He slept on the prayer mats and ate the free food from those who needed to reward the people who prayed for them.

He listened to the holy men sing:
My beloved has returned.
Allah has united us.

And the supplicants moved their heads to the beat of the *dhol*. Some came with boxes of sweets, chicken, and goats covered with henna; others came with garlands of hundreds of rupee notes, a whole year's income. Anything to get their prayers heard. The maulvi sat and prayed for two long weeks, not wanting to return to the comfort of his wife until his own prayer was acknowledged.

Now, miracle of miracles, his prayers from those twenty

years earlier had been answered that morning. With both hands, he picked up the baby. Covered with afterbirth, she was still connected to Tara, and he held her close to his heart. He dipped his right hand in the canal and very gently wiped her face. He took his turban off his head with the same damp hand and struggled to wrap it around the baby. He could see her heart pumping in her tiny body. He would make sure she survived.

Enraptured, he spoke to Shahida. "You're late, but you're here. You should have told us you were coming. I would have done some preparation. I'll get you a doll, a plastic one from the stalls at the shrine, one that looks just like you."

She no longer called to the disappearing star as he continued to talk to her.

"I'll cook two cauldrons of goat meat for the whole village. I'll announce to everyone that my princess has arrived. Your mother is waiting for you at home. You're a sly one, aren't you? Coming without an announcement."

The baby started to whimper again as they sat waiting for help to arrive. Her tiny hand reached out to us, asking us to continue to protect her, as we had done all that night. We were assured she would live.

Communal Obligation

W e, the flies, hovered over the maulvi and Baby Shahida for three hours before the milkman returned with a horse-cart owner and a woman sitting in the back seat. It was midmorning, and the heat covered us like a shroud.

The maulvi saw his neighbor Hamida's mother alight from the cart. Overcome by the sight of Tara and the maulvi holding the baby still attached to her dead mother, she steadied herself and then threw up. It took her some time to separate the mother from her child, and then the cart driver and the milkman wrapped Tara's body in a bedsheet that Hamida's mother had brought with her and placed her on the cart.

Hamida's mother took the baby from the maulvi, and the pallbearing cart returned to the village, leaving the maulvi walking slowly behind, not yet knowing that he would be leading not only Tara's funeral prayers that day, but also Bhaggan's.

Maria had found Bhaggan's body that morning when she had arrived to help with the housework. She ran to tell Saffiya about it, and as she returned with Saffiya to Bhaggan's room, she saw the wretchedly slow horse-cart procession enter the front yard.

"Call your father, daughter!" said the maulvi, now breathless from the morning's exertion. "He needs to go to the cane field. Tara is no longer with us, and Maalik needs to be told."

We, the flies, lingered above the cart and the maulvi, and we saw Maria's already swollen eyes overcome with the sorrow that would cause her to implode if she spent a moment more standing there. We flew toward her, and she blew us away as she walked toward her home, choosing not to share her own devastating news about Bhaggan with the maulvi. He would soon find out.

We had seen Maria as a baby, cared for by Tara and Bhaggan. Now she walked with strength that we could never have imagined as she left the house to tell her father what the maulvi needed him to do.

When Maria left, Saffiya stood at the front door, leaning on the handle, while the milkman lifted Tara's body off the cart and placed her carefully on the charpoy at the entrance.

Saffiya barely glanced at Tara, concealing her devastation by busying herself with arranging for the three-day prayer session to ensure the ascent to paradise of the souls of the two women who had been closer to her than anyone else in the village.

She looked at the baby with tearless sorrow. Her legs trembled, and she reached for a chair to steady herself.

"Allah will care for this one," she said mournfully, and then, more practically, "Take her to Zakia. Her lap has been empty for so long. She will care for her."

Hamida's mother held the baby, wrapped in a threadbare towel, close to her. Reluctantly, she walked toward the maulvi's house.

We, the flies, hovered over Maria and Isaac, sitting on the back seat of the horse cart as they drove to the cane field, where they found Maalik lying, staring into the fields, waiting for the boar to reappear. Maria let out a wail, which ended abruptly as her father wrapped his arm around her.

The cart driver turned to Isaac. "Help me lift him, brother, or he'll not live much longer."

Isaac had already sat Maria down and reached for his shoulder cloth to wipe Maalik's face. The cart driver pulled the cotton blanket from the charpoy to lift Maalik without causing more harm.

Instead of taking him back to Saffiya's, they took Maalik to the hospital, where Stella assisted the nurses. Maalik's external wounds would take a year to heal, but the scars they left went deep inside him and were permanent.

IN THE FIRST few years of Maalik's horror, Maria made many attempts to crack the hard shell he had grown to protect himself, but she was unable to break through his tortured mantle. As if his armor protected him from his horrendous past and his unknown future. As hard as Maria tried, Maalik would never be able to comprehend what had happened to Bhaggan and Tara. And he would never know that his daughter, Shahida, had been born and was being cared for by the maulvi and his wife, Zakia.

Unfortunately for Shahida, Zakia had replaced her thirst for motherhood with a passion for the prayer rug and the Quran. For twenty years, the rhythms and rituals of prayer had soothed the anxiety of childlessness and helped her get through the long, empty days. Now, when she was gifted with Baby Shahida, she couldn't find the love that had dissipated with the death of her own babies. And so Shahida began her young life with an aging mother who had no understanding of how to care for the infant she had been waiting for all those years.

Zakia took Shahida in her arms, but Shahida cried for the first six months without stopping. The maulvi picked her up and carried her around, but still she found no peace. They tried all kinds of herbal remedies, but nothing worked. They barely slept in all those months, and then, as if sensing her adoptive parents' exhaustion, six-month-old Shahida stopped crying and started to stare. She looked at everyone who passed by her cloth swing hanging from the side of Zakia's charpoy. She never cried, but nor did she laugh.

When the wheat was being harvested again, the following year, she started to walk. Shahida was now a year old, and we, the flies, stayed with her, as we were beholden. She just stood up one day from her crawl and began to run toward the maulvi when he entered at night. He was so pleased to see her walk that he took her to the shrine.

We, the flies, flew around her while, on her first visit to the shrine, she began to dance to the drumbeats. She danced so long that the maulvi had to pick her up, and then she started to cry again. The maulvi, seeing Shahida's joy at the shrine, kept returning with her. Soon he realized that this was the only place where she seemed content, and so, as she grew older, he took her there weekly.

Zakia never came to the shrine. She had decided that her prayers were heard directly from the prayer mat, which was now worn out where she stood, and on the domes of the mosque where she placed her forehead in supplication, and in wanting the *zebibah* mark of piety from having been in constant supplication.

The shrine, with its beggars at the gate and its drummers and *qawals* on Thursdays, was not a place for women. The women who went to the shrine were of ill repute, and Zakia never wanted to be associated with them.

She also couldn't understand her husband's obsession with the place. She had plenty to do at home now that Hamida had gotten married and left the village, and Nafissa came only some days to help her old teacher, but she would also be married soon. Zakia would have to find someone else to help her with the chores.

"Why do you take her there?" Zakia asked her husband while he combed Shahida's hair, parting it on one side. He placed a hat on her head as if she were a little boy. Then he carried her to the shrine on his shoulders.

Zakia couldn't have known that Shahida was happiest there. "I'll bring her back by evening prayers," he responded, with no further explanation. And Zakia continued preparing the dough for that night's meal, covering her head with her chador to avoid white hairs in the bread.

Shahida perched silently on her father's shoulders, looking at the world from her new height. "Take my shoulder cloth and cover your head to avoid the heat and the flies," the maulvi would tell her when she started to understand what he said. But we, the flies who hovered around them, were her friends, and we danced with her when she danced to the music at the shrine.

My beloved has come home. Tell the clock keeper to stop keeping time, the supplicants sang at the shrine.

And in the tender times at night when the maulvi lay down with his wife as Shahida slept in the room next door, he would say to Zakia, "I want the clock to stop now. I want to carry Shahida to the shrine on my shoulders forever. I want to see her dance forever. I want to hear her laugh."

Not knowing how Shahida changed in her happiness at the shrine, Zakia would turn over and go to sleep, oblivious to how the future would unfold for them.

❦

AS SHAHIDA GREW older, she and the maulvi continued to visit the shrine, holding hands down the noisy path. She would stare at the sputtering motorcycle slowed down by a family of six perched precariously on top, leaving an exhausting trail of dust behind. The growls of starving dogs fighting over a bone thrown out by the butcher distracted her, but the maulvi tugged at her tiny arm, leading her toward the shrine. And we, the flies, danced around them as they approached their destination.

Whenever the maulvi had a few extra coins, Shahida got to distribute them among the beggars at the entrance to the shrine. She would place the paisa in each child's bowl. When she looked up at her father for more, he would tell her, "Next time. Now we should find our place near the drummers and singers."

Shahida held his hand tightly, and he held it even more tightly, saving her from the crush of supplicants. We had seen children older than she bundled away and mutilated or blinded to stand with the beggars and gather coins. The maulvi protected her from such a fate.

The maulvi and Zakia pulled her in opposite directions. When she was old enough to read, Zakia tried to teach her the Qaida, as she had done for Tara and all the other village children. But Shahida would rather play with us, the flies. This infuriated Zakia, and, to save Shahida from her ire, the maulvi took her to the shrine even more often.

Shahida continued to grow into her own during this tug-of-war between her parents. The chaotic world of the shrine became the space that she made her own. Her mother, Tara, whom we, the flies, had protected all those years, had not found such belonging in her short life. Shahida had found her Self and her home by the time she was twelve.

For twelve years, the maulvi and Shahida continued this way, until Shahida asked her father if they could stay the night at the shrine. He knew he had no other choice but to consent. He also knew he'd have to deal with Zakia's anger about this development when he returned.

Once they had crossed that boundary, Shahida was able to convince her old father that she could stay at the shrine without him, first one night, and then another, until she had no reason to return to her home in the village. Over time, she would make the shrine her home, never to leave it again.

By the time she was twelve, the devotees at the shrine venerated her for the blessings she brought with her. They, in return, brought her gifts, and as she sang and danced to the drumbeat, they begged her to pray for them, and she did, and they kept returning to the shrine, bringing gifts of goats to slaughter.

Atonement

Twelve years after Tara and Bhaggan died and Shahida was born, Saffiya lived on.

Maalik lived, too, as did Maria and Stella. A few months after the tragedy, Jannat passed on, and Maria left her father in the village and joined her sister, Stella, in the hospital. Unlike her sister, she never learned to read or write, but the nuns hired her to clean the hospital wards.

Maria's life in the village had prepared her to care for others. She used this skill with Maalik, who stayed in the hospital because he had no reason to return to the village. Stella had convinced the nuns to make the ward his permanent home.

As she cared for him, Maria tried to remind him about Tara, hoping he might retain those happy memories. But they had been erased, along with those of his brothers and his mother. She wanted him to know that he had a daughter, and she tried to remind him that he had a brother, Taaj, who might be living in another city. But none of this interested him. He found no consolation in what she shared with him.

We, the flies, knew better. We knew that Maalik was already lost in a world from which he would never return.

❧

FIVE YEARS AFTER the tragedy, Taaj found his way back home and learned from Saffiya all that had happened. He came to the hospital to visit Maalik. He met with Maria and Stella. They huddled around Maalik, remembering the past and at times daring to laugh at memories that seemed so distant. Maalik stayed aloof, spending his days sitting on the hospital bed, venturing out only when Maria or Stella coerced him. Then he would sit on the charpoy outside the hospital entrance, staring at the horse carts and buses driving by.

Taaj had never accomplished what he had anticipated when he had run away from the village. His life in the city was neither better nor worse. But he began visiting his brother and his two childhood friends regularly. As a day laborer, he never had enough work, so he would join them at the hospital. He made just enough to survive. And when he came, he smoked bidis with his brother, reminiscing about the past that Maalik could not remember.

"Maybe if he went to the shrine," Maria said to her sister, Stella, who had never been to the shrine and couldn't understand how that would help. "Tara and I went there once with Amman Bhaggan. We bought dolls from there." She smiled as she remembered that time. "And Maulvi says that Shahida has made it her home. If Maalik goes there, he will see her. He might even bring her back."

We, the flies, knew that none of these desires Maria harbored could help Maalik. He no longer had the capacity to deal with the past. He was barely surviving the present.

"Taaj must take him to the shrine when he comes next." Maria was adamantly optimistic.

At first, Taaj was reluctant to do what Maria asked when

he arrived on a Thursday. Maria, however, was not going to give up. It wasn't long before he chose to leave her at the hospital, wanting to take full responsibility for helping his brother find peace.

On Thursdays, the shrine of Sain Makhianwala, the Keeper of Flies, crawled with supplicants. The dying, the close-to-dying, and those wanting death for themselves or for others came with offerings to accentuate their prayers, bringing sacrificial goats, chickens, and sometimes even a buffalo if the need was great, like that of a large dowry or a rich son-in-law, and especially one with a small family.

Sugar balls were all that Taaj could afford to intensify his prayers. Somehow, Maria pulled together enough money for the bus trip but not enough for the gift for the shrine.

We, the flies, hovered over the brothers. Taaj steadied Maalik when the bus took off before they had fully alighted.

As soon as they arrived at the shrine, beggars surrounded the two young men. A coin slipped through Taaj's fingers, falling soundlessly, rolling past the goat droppings, disappearing under torn newspaper stained with grease from spicy fries. Taaj looked longingly at the lost coin, hoping it was the ten-paisa piece and not fifty paisas.

Mistaking the brothers for beggars, the shrine keeper gave them roti and some daal, which they ate, and then they slept on the bare charpoys provided to supplicants who chose to stay the night at the shrine.

The two brothers slept soundly, as if they were huddled on the charpoy outside Bhaggan's room. They slept as if their brother, Sultan, were asleep on a charpoy next to them. We, the flies, settled on Maalik's chest. We heard it beat, and we sensed his peace. We sensed the pleasure of the young man dreaming of his beloved, Tara. Of the day he married her. As if, in his dreams, everyone were still alive. In his dreams, everything that happened unfolded the way he had wanted it to, not the way it had really happened.

We sensed his heartbeat accelerating to the drumbeat of his dreams, as if the village women sang in praise of the young man.

The king of nations, my father's beloved.

The support of my mother's heart; my brother ascends the white horse.

And we sensed his body stiffen, as if he dreamed of walking upright toward a white horse, to Saffiya's house, to collect his beloved, Tara. He turned his gaze, as if to admire his brother's dance to the beat of the hired drummer, and his mother, throwing rupee notes to ward off the evil eye from her handsome young sons.

He smiled as if he dreamed of pulling aside the strands of roses tied to his forehead to view his bride. The lover in search of his beloved, with whom he would unite by the end of the day. The day of his dreams since he had first sensed the smell of her beautiful, thick braid, seen her laughing eyes, and beheld her luscious lips.

And then Taaj awoke but his brother still slept beside him, and we, the flies, swarmed around.

Taaj stared at the *dhamal* dancers at the shrine as they stamped their feet and swung their heads, men and women together. The dancing continued until the early hours of dawn. Then he whispered to anyone who could hear, "Water. Can someone give me some water?"

A little beggar girl passed him an earthenware bowl full of water and then pulled him through a small crowd around the banyan tree to the right of the shrine. He drank as if his thirst could never be quenched.

Shrouded in a patched green cassock, Shahida sat cross-legged, oblivious to her surroundings. In front of her was a brightly colored basket filled with white sugar balls, offerings from her devotees.

We, the flies, circumnavigated the sugar pile seven times before landing. Within a few seconds, we draped the white heap of sugar balls with darkness.

Shahida looked down at us but chose not to look at the young man in front of her and recited:

A drop of ink on a white sheet.

Taaj leaned forward, listening to Shahida, and she continued.

Layla is exquisite like the night.
Her dark beauty is invisible to you.

Taaj swayed his head in understanding. Shahida continued to ignore him, but Taaj was now lost in the depth of her words.

We, the flies, saw Maalik awaken, stand, and stretch. We saw his searching eyes, and we saw his acknowledgment as he turned around and returned to his life, leaving his brother, Taaj, at the shrine.

Shahida nodded, then swung her head back, reflecting the starlight in her eyes.

We, the flies, spiraled toward the starlight. Shahida and we became one.

Oblivious to the squalor and stench, Shahida slipped over the devotees before her, swiftly, racing the sunrise over the alfalfa fields, skimming the rising steam.

Elongated by the setting moon, her shadow melted into the fumes of dung cakes beside the river where the buffalo stood sleeping. She hovered over the mangy street dog still searching for his soul but flew rapidly on toward the mud hut in the middle of the cane field.

Her brief life as one of us would soon end, to begin again on the still-damp dung cakes or on some rotting fruit, but before that happened, she would reach her destination.

Her exhausted wings dragged, but as long as she saw the movement around her, she kept going. As a fly, she could transcend space and time.

During the flight, the past became the present and she was no longer twelve; she was not yet born. She was yet to emerge from her mother. To live and relive each moment of ecstasy.

About the Author

Anniqua Rana lives in California with her husband and two sons. When she's not working as an educator in the community college system, she visits her family in Pakistan and England. The rest of the time, she reads, cooks, travels, and enjoys mystical music and poetry and does whatever it takes to keep her grounded and happy.